## MORE PRAISE FOR
## *THE LIGHT BETWEEN THE PINES*

"Read's novel is a quiet, deep character study of a man reckoning with his mistakes and shortcomings in a continuing effort to right his relationship with his daughter. In a novel that's straightforward and steeped in reflections about place, Red is a fully realized character as he thinks "he understood now the expectation of silence in a place like this, among people like these. The pull between what a person should do versus what they had to do."—*KIRKUS*

"Warren Read is as good as any writer I know at getting under the skin of his characters, especially those who'd prefer to keep people out. Red Miller is a reluctant detective and even more reluctant sharer of his feelings, but he feels deeply, and while he searches for his missing daughter, we feel with him as if she's our own. T*he Light Between the Pines* is a gripping and gorgeous novel about the lengths parents go to look out for their wayward children, even those beyond their help, and a community that does whatever it can to protect its most vulnerable members."
—SCOTT NADELSON, author of *Trust Me*, and *While it Lasts*

"In *The Light Between the Pines*, we are thrust into the tense, prickly relationship between Red and his daughter Gina. The stakes are high. One wrong move, and he will lose her. This beautifully wrought novel explores themes of family and resilience, as well as possible redemption. We believe in the "curious gift" of family as well as the renewal Red barely dared to believe in. A wonderful story."
—JESSICA BARKSDALE INCLÁN, author of *What the Moon Did* and *What They Found at the Lake*

I0805517

# THE LIGHT BETWEEN THE PINES

# THE LIGHT BETWEEN THE PINES

WARREN READ

PUBLISHING

New York, NY

This is a work of fiction. Names, characters, businesses, places, events and incidents are either the products of the author's imagination or used in a fictitious manner. Any resemblance to actual persons, living or dead, or actual events is purely coincidental.



Ig Publishing, Inc.
Box 2547
New York, NY 10163
www.igpub.com

ISBN: 978-1-63246-213-8

Printed in the United States of America
First US edition
Manufactuer: Lightning Source

*For my mother, and a lifetime of stories.*

# EARLY FALL, 1979

# 1

Red Miller stood on his front porch and watched Frankie, his daughter's newish boyfriend, lean against the railing and light up another cigarette, using the cherry of the one he'd just drawn down almost to the filter. The railing was weak and sun-cooked, and it gave a little under the kid's weight, even though he was scrawny as one of the spindles behind him. The thing had been begging for a repair since last season, and now all Red could do was imagine that any minute it might just give way and send the young man ass over teakettle, straight into the rosebushes.

He nodded at Frankie's hip and warned him. "Watch that railing."

Frankie turned to look down at his seat before stepping off and snapping the old filter from his fingers out onto the lawn. "That'd be something," he said.

"You ain't kidding," Red quipped.

Frankie had been running with Gina going on a few months, and even though this boy was too old for her—twenty-four to Gina's just-turned-eighteen—it wasn't the first time the math had been lopsided with her. There wasn't a hell of a lot Red or anyone else could do about it, Gina being so headstrong and shortsighted as a goat. Frankie seemed to ground her a bit, make her less prone to drama and crisis. And from what Red could tell, he didn't appear to be the hitting kind.

Frankie reached into his jeans' pocket and took out a stack of twenties, folded in the middle. He counted out six of them and handed them over to Red.

"I do appreciate it," Frankie said. "Saved us."

Red tucked the bills into his shirt pocket. While they'd all agreed that the last thing any of them needed was a kid to mix things up, Red was surprised at just how unexpectedly cold the cash felt against his chest. It was as if something more should be said about it, now that it was all over and done with. But what? There was nothing to say that hadn't already been said.

Gina kept herself away from the conversation with her back to them both, way the hell at the edge of the lawn, near the car. Red wondered how in the world this fellow had lasted as long as he had with her—Gina with her hair burned out yellow, a shirt so loose on her little frame it was likely she'd pulled it from the boy's closet that morning. Red worried that it was only a matter of time until there would indeed be a little one running up and down that sidewalk, wailing like a banshee and drawing the cocked heads of crows perched on the fence line.

"How's the car holding up?" Red asked. The Valiant had been his late wife's car, only recently brought out of the garage into the daylight, draped under a decade's worth of dust and cobwebs. After recovering the missing distributor cap and taking the long weekend to get the thing running again, Red had handed it over to Gina on her birthday. It was what Gretchen would have wanted, he told himself. When he presented the car to Gina, he snapped a Polaroid of her leaning against the hood. She rolled her eyes as she watched the image come into view.

"Gross," she moaned. "I never take good pictures."

"I like it," Red told her. "I like the smile."

She gave him a quick hug, awkward as always, and he tucked the snapshot into his shirt pocket. Later, after she'd driven off, he stuck it onto the refrigerator door with a strip of painter's tape.

"She's running decent," Frankie said. "Pulls a little to the left, but not bad." He looked down at his shoes and chewed on his lip a bit. The edges of a tattoo pushed up from his buttoned shirt, the tips of outstretched wings nearly reaching his collarbone. He seemed to be hanging on to something else.

"What is it?" Red asked. He didn't know this Frankie fellow enough that it was a normal thing for the two of them to be standing there on the porch together, shooting the breeze about anything. Clearly the kid wanted something.

"The thing is," Frankie said, "we're a bit shy this month."

Here it was.

"On rent and such. Expenses, you know."

Red leaned to one side to try and catch Frankie's eye, but the kid wouldn't have it. It had been like that since the two of them met, Red doing what he could to forge even a little bit of connection. Anything to bridge the gap between where he stood and his own daughter.

"A bit shy," Red said with a laugh. He pulled the twenties from his shirt pocket and handed them back. Frankie's face flushed as he took the bills.

"It's the last time, sir," he stammered. "I promise."

Red took the promise with a nod of his head. A promise as empty as his shirt pocket. "Some might say the two of you have created a tough situation for yourselves."

Frankie was watching Gina as she sat down on the edge of the lawn and started picking tufts of grass from the dirt. "We're all right," he said. "Most of the time. I got work doing security down at the casino."

"That's good to hear." Red knew Gina could hear them as she brushed her hand over the tips of the grass, pretending she was miles away from it all.

Frankie glanced at Red quickly, the ghost of a smile on the edge of his mouth. "Mister Miller," he said, as if reading Red's mind. "With all due respect, you know why I'm the one that's up here and not her."

Of course Red knew. An ask from Gina would tumble out like an expectation. And in no time the whole thing would leverage into a fight, a single question posed by Red spun by her into some unreasonable interrogation. He watched Frankie light up a new cigarette and draw from it, his reddened eyes squinting with the movement as Gina stood up and walked back and forth along the edge of the lawn, scraping at it with her shoe.

"So, is that it, then?" Red asked. He leaned forward, resting his hand on the railing. "Anything else you both need?"

"The cash will do just great," Frankie said, shifting himself so he blocked Red's line of sight to his daughter. "I do appreciate it, Mister Miller," he said. "We both do."

Red considered Frankie's words and accepted them to be as true as they could be. He leaned to one side and there was Gina, leaning over the hood of the car now, rubbing at something with her thumb.

"You're welcome," Red called over.

She spun to look at him, her cottony hair falling over her shoulder like the hem of a dress. Her face had the response he'd expected—mouth drawn open, brow furrowed—as if someone had suggested she might have killed somebody.

"I was gonna say thank you," she hollered back. "If you gave me a minute."

Red felt the familiar crawling over his hands and feet, the kind of anxiousness that his daughter was so skilled at bringing out. He clenched his jaw and drew in a breath of air, slowly.

"Besides the rent," he said, "everything else okay?"

"Yeah, it's alright," Frankie said. "If things go good at the casino I'll get a twenty cent an hour raise. My ninety-day review comes up next month."

"What about her?" Red pressed, nodding toward Gina with his chin. "Any headway happening with the GED?"

Frankie looked at him with eyelids half-mast, the cigarette hanging from his lip like it had fallen in place accidentally. "Not that I know of," he said. "She'll be okay, though." He pinched his smoke and sucked hard so that the cherry ran almost halfway down. He let out a stream of blue, and the smoke rolled between the two of them, hanging there until Frankie waved it off with his hand. "We'll both be okay."

Gina folded her arms across her chest and walked over to the porch. She had gone and put a second earring in her ear, this one a little loop up near the top. It was right there, catching the sunlight just so, as if she was daring Red to say something about it.

"I got the flu," she said. "Last week. I was sick as a dog."

"The flu's no fun," Red said. "You can get a shot, you know."

"I know."

"Too late now, though."

She narrowed her eyes at him, cocked her head, and shifted her weight from one foot to the other. He could see she was processing. Turning things over in that head of hers.

"Well, I'm glad you're better," Red offered. "You look healthy."

"Yeah, well..." Her face relaxed some. "It's almost three

o'clock" she said to Frankie. Then to Red: "We got a picnic we're going to. Some friends over at Lake Goodwin."

"You have a good time," Red said. "It was nice to see you."

"You too," Gina said. She waved to him behind her back as she walked to the car and got into the passenger side.

"She can be a tough one," Frankie said. He held his hand out. "Thank you again, Mr. Miller for the money. For everything, really. I promise we'll pay you back as soon as we can."

"All right, then," Red said, shaking his hand.

The horn issued a hard reminder, and Frankie gave a start. "Well," he said, "you know how she is." He snapped the last of his cigarette out onto the grass then stepped the long walkway down to the car. And then they were both gone, nothing but a few cigarette butts in the rose bed and a spot of oil black against the curb to show that they were ever there to begin with.

# MIDSUMMER, 1984

# 2

Red was deep into the engine compartment of Molly Conway's '63 Fairlane, one knee propped on the bumper as the heat of the trouble light warmed his neck. His hands were caked in black, and the new fuel pump waited on the garage floor, resting on the morning's sports section. Though the door to the house was closed, he could still hear the phone ringing from where he was in the shop.

He climbed out of the car and went on up to the house, pushing open the front door at the exact moment the answering machine kicked in. His voice tumbled through the house, deep and gravelly, too much like his father's to stand listening to for long.

Hello, this is the Miller house and I'm not here.

He headed to the kitchen and ambled over to the sink, turning on the water and running his hands under the stream before giving them a good dusting of Ajax, scrubbing them together into a thick, ashy paste.

The greeting on the machine came to an end with a sharp tone, followed by a good deal of static and then what sounded like a person caught in a fit of heavy coughing. Red shut off the water and looked through the doorway that opened into the living room. The answering machine sat where it always did, on the side table, next to the sofa. A bead of green light stared at him. Finally, a voice clipped out, sharp as the knock of a mallet against a drum.

"This message is for Red Miller. Mr. Miller, this is deputy Len Brody of the Kootenai County Sheriff's department. Idaho."

Here it was again. Only this time, Idaho.

"When you get a chance, I'd like very much to talk with you."

Red sighed and took a few steps away from the sink but then stopped, resting a hand on the counter. The tile was cold against his callused skin. Sunlight pushed through the window blinds and filled the space with yellow stripes, tiny specks of dust moving slowly through the air as if the room was breathing.

"It's regarding one Gina Miller." Again, a cough and then a heavy breath of air, labored. Finally, the man rattled off a phone number and said, again, "When you get a chance, please."

Red pulled a chair from beneath the kitchen table and sank down into it. The gray Formica and chrome set had been a fixture in his kitchen for almost thirty years. He'd bought it for his mother as a gift when he came home from the army. The cigarette burn under his thumb was like a Braille message, a permanent reminder of her last days, when she would sit at this table in her own kitchen, defiantly smoking in spite of the little tube running into her nose and the spreading blackness in her lungs.

Red leaned back and looked out the window. He told himself it was nothing more than the usual. A warrant. An unpleasant domestic situation, perhaps. A five-finger discount from some department store. But there was, as always, the nagging possibility that this might finally be the one—*The Call*—and that's what pulled on him. The punctuation mark at the end of what had been a never-ending sentence with her. His heart drummed in his chest, and then came the familiar burn behind his eyes.

The sun was just touching the rooftops across the street, a glowing circle saddled smartly between two peaks. It was almost orange, ripe and dark, with a thin veil of clouds brushed over it. July hadn't even finished, and already things were beginning to feel like fall to him. It was hard to count on any kind of truth anymore.

It had been five years since he'd laid eyes on her, since that day she took off with that fellow Frankie. Gina had been perched in the driver's seat of the smoke-filled Valiant, gazing at Red with that toothy grin of hers, behind the grime of too much lipstick. She'd be back the following week to repay him, she said. Red knew he'd have a better chance of winning the lottery than ever seeing that cash again.

As weeks ran into months, and then years, and there was one thing after the other, from one place to another, Red came to accept that there would likely come a day when the phone would ring and that'd be it. Yet, with the exception of a single call from a furious landlord looking for someone to honor a bad check, the law had been quiet when it came to her. Instead, most of the calls had been from Gina herself, a plea for bail money or maybe someone from a collection agency, or an ex-boyfriend trying to track her down. And so there would be a kind of wash that would come over him once the fog lifted, a numbing feeling, as if he'd downed a double shot of whiskey. It was what she did and was good at—get herself into some kind of bind and then work his heart every which way she could. There were too many times he felt crushed under the shame of wanting to just erase everything, all those moments when he fought the urge to make that return call. Stay out of the fray, he'd learned to tell himself. How many times had it gone the way he'd hoped it would? Like water on a rock—the constant drip eventually wears it all down.

Red lifted himself up from the chair as the machine clicked, both moments happening simultaneously, as if one had caused the other. He stood for a few minutes without moving, sensing the way the deputy's voice seemed to hang in the room, like the dust still huddling in the last shafts of sunlight. He took a quick glance at the old Polaroid on the fridge, of Gina and the Valiant, and then at last he went from the kitchen to the living room, to the machine that now blinked green at him. He pressed his thumb over the button and erased the message, removing it from the space as if it had never come.

As he walked to the back bedroom to change out of his greasy clothes, he passed by the collage of frames, a wall jumbled with black and white grammar school portraits of Gina, and snapshots from the long July road trip to Yellowstone that he and Gretchen had taken her on, and of the sweltering picnic on the edge of Canyon River. There were the Girl Scout patches and her Christening certificate, and the photo of her and Gretchen standing with arms entwined beside the leaning snowman they had dressed in Red's father's old Panama, one of the few things of his he had anymore. Where, he wondered, had he been in all of these? Why hadn't anyone thought to put him and Gina inside a frame?

Now, though, it was getting too dark to see any of it. Now it was nothing but a collage of faceless shapes and shadows that lined the long hallway to the back of a house that was simply too big for one man.

# 3

There were two men shooting pool when Red came in through the back door, young fellows he didn't know though he recognized them from their little beards and their haircuts, short on the top and long in the back like confused girls. They nodded at him, and he tapped his fingers to his forehead in a courtesy salute. From the looks of things, they weren't too far into their game, balls still all over the table. It wasn't often that you had to wait to play on a Tuesday evening, but Red wasn't in any kind of rush.

"Give me a holler when it's open," he said, dropping a pair of quarters on the wood. He walked over to the bar, ordered a beer, then headed through the smoke to the openness of the tavern area and the breeze of the overhead fan. There was a good song going on the jukebox, one of those old doo-wop groups that Red could never keep straight. The Platters or the Four Tops, maybe. The kind of music he liked to fall asleep to as a teenager, drifting softly through his radio long after his parents thought he'd gone off to bed. It felt good to hear it just now.

Linda Foss was at their usual table by the window, nursing a beer. She'd gotten her hair trimmed some since Red last saw her. It was just over her shoulders now, a little short but still all right.

She looked over at him and smiled, and the way she pulled one side of her hair from her face, it seemed to him that she might expect him to say something to her about it.

"I was starting to figure you weren't coming," Linda said. She slid out from the table and came to him and wrapped her arms around his waist, pressing a quick kiss to his lips. Linda was a good-sized woman, round in the hips and breasts in a way that Red liked just fine, though that roundness did bother her at times. She liked to go on about how, when she worked for the forestry department years earlier, she would spend her days hiking the trails. "I was in damned good shape then," she'd say. "You should have seen me."

"I like the shape you are now," Red would say, and Linda would slap at him and blush.

"You got a haircut," he said.

She smiled and brushed the bangs from her forehead. "I got all of 'em cut," she said, winking at him.

"I can tell."

She tipped her head to one side and screwed up her mouth. "So what? You don't like it?"

"Oh, it's a real fine cut. Let's me see your face a little better."

Red sat down next to the window and looked outside, but there was nothing to see in the dark but streetlamps and the taillights of cars leaving the parking lot. Linda took the seat across from him and pushed her knees up against his and held them there. She stared at him for a few moments and Red could feel her searching, looking for the cracks he refused to show.

"Give me your hands," she said, reaching out. Red laid his hands out on the table and she picked them up then turned them over. She clicked her tongue. "Spic and span," she said. "No work today?"

"Plenty of work," Red answered. "Did a set of brake pads for the cousin of a buddy of mine. I also got going on a fuel pump for old Molly Conway out there on River Road. You know her?"

"Yeah, I know her." Linda grinned and showed her teeth, the gold one on the right side peeking through. "She used to do my mom's hair back when she still had the salon there on Main Street. They had a falling out, though."

"Falling out? What set that off? She seems like an easy kind of gal to me."

"She's a gal who doesn't always think about what she says to who."

Red slid his hands back and tucked them onto his lap. "I guess I've not seen that side of her. Could be your mother brought it out of her?"

Linda smiled and showed her gold tooth again. "Red Miller, you better watch what you say about my mama. She put up with an awful lot in her day."

Red winked at her, then leaned back in his seat and took a drink of his beer. Maybe Molly did step too much into places that weren't her business. She always had stories to tell whenever she came by, but Red didn't typically pay them any mind. Hell, people probably said things about him and Linda, pegging what they had as something more or less than it was. There was no doubt folks likely had a few ideas about Gretchen at one point. And Gina.

"I saved us a spot at the pool table," Red said. "If you're up for a game."

"I might be," she said.

"I promise to go easy on you," he smiled.

They sipped beer between small talk and glances at the football game on the television set and pretty soon Red forgot about the pool table. More than once, he lost track of what Linda was saying, and found himself scrambling to fill in the gaps. There were too many moments when that phone call intruded on his thoughts, the way the officer had said "One Gina Miller." One, as if she was a single among many, and he didn't know what that could mean.

"Red!" Linda snapped her fingers.

"Yeah?"

"What's going on with you?"

He turned to look back at the television, as if there could be something on the screen that might show a way out. Finally, he just waved a hand as if he was brushing away a fly.

"Don't give me that," Linda said. She leaned forward with her elbows on the table. "You got the attention span of a squirrel over there. I want to know what's on your mind."

"Nothing, hon. Just a long day is all."

"You've never been one to lie to me, Red. Please don't start now."

When he didn't answer, she slid back in her seat and put her hands on her lap. Her shoulders sank. "You losing interest? Is that what it is?"

"Hell no," he said.

"It's fine, Red. Just level with me is all, so I don't come out of this looking like a fool."

He reached over the table and held his hand out until she took hold of it. He closed his fingers over hers and they looked at each other for a good length of time without saying anything. When he smiled at her she smiled back. When he squeezed her hand, she lifted it to her cheek and pressed it against her skin.

"Some cop called the house today," Red said. "Gina." The way he had to force himself to say her name, he may as well have been calling out a stranger.

"Is she all right?"

"Christ, I don't know. Likely. It's always something; you know that. If not one thing, it's another. My guess is she's either in jail again or near to it." Red caught the waitress's eye and held up two fingers. He then leaned back into his seat and rubbed his palms over his eyes, which stung under the rolling pressure.

"Don't hide behind those hands of yours," Linda said. "Talk to me."

He laid his fists on the table and waited for her face to come into focus again, and the worry in her eyes was at once reassuring and painful. "I don't know," he said. "As much as I feel like I'm nothing but calluses when it comes to her anymore, it still finds a way in."

"She's your daughter," Linda said. "A lousy friend can grind you up until you're nothing but dust. But then you can let go. But your kid? No matter how hard they work on you, there's always a little pebble in there that's worth trying to save." Linda held her gaze on Red, what he always called pity tracks drawn down to her temples. Neither of them said anything further for a while. The waitress came over with the beers and put them down on the table. They each took a good drink from their bottles. Finally, Linda said, "You're gonna call him back, right? The deputy?"

"I imagine I will eventually."

Linda put her hands on the table. "I don't wanna stick my nose where it doesn't belong, Red, but you ought to at least find out what the hell is going on."

He let out an exhausted sigh. "I'm sure it's nothing," he said.

"You don't even sound convinced yourself."

"Honey, you don't know what it's like to go months without hearing a single goddamn thing from her and then out of the blue she or someone else calls me up with some kind of emergency.

Money to pay a ticket or she's gonna lose her car, or God knows what. Some cop from Boondocks, Idaho calls me and I'm supposed to just jump up and fix everything all over again. I'm telling you it's nothing but games with Gina, and I'm not playing them anymore. She's an adult, goddamn it."

"I hear you, Red."

"It's taken me a long time to get here. I know it sounds cold, but if I let myself fall back into it..."

Linda reached out and took his hand in hers. "I know a thing or two about codependence and boundaries and everything in between," she said. "Believe me. I just wondered if you might want to call him back. If only to see what it's all about, that's all."

Something happened on the television and a group of folks whooped and cheered. An old codger at one end of the bar raised a fist in the air and hollered, "Get your money out, mister," and a guy at the other end said, "Don't you get your girdle in a pinch Oscar, it ain't over till it's over."

Linda took another drink from her bottle and set it down. "I've given my two cents and now I'm gonna shut my mouth about it. You do what you think is best." And the way she said this to him, her eyes and her voice rock steady, her knees pressed hard against his, made Red feel a kind of shift inside. As if a puzzle piece had been snapped perfectly into place.

And then the outside door opened behind them, and a rush of fresh air spilled into the place. A figure stood in the doorway, hat in hand, scanning the room. When his head moved to face Red and Linda, it stopped.

"Red Miller." It was Will Harrigan, the deputy under Sheriff Slater. He walked over to their booth and stood over them. He looked at Red, his bushy, wild eyebrows pulled down at the sides, lips pressed into a straight line. "Some fellow over in Idaho been trying to track you down. He called us about an hour ago."

"I'm sorry you got pulled into whatever it is," Red said. Behind the deputy, the young fellows playing pool laid their cues on the table. One of them looked over to Red and gave him a nod, but Red waved him off.

Harrigan said, "Just doing my job." He looked at Linda. "Can we talk in private, Red? Step outside for a minute?"

Linda reached across the table and took a firm hold on Red's wrist.

Only when he felt just how warm her skin was against his did Red realize that all of the blood had left his hands.

# 4

As he talked to Deputy Harrigan, Red could see the shape of Linda's face at the tavern window, watching the two of them beside his truck. He wouldn't expect anything less from her.

"They found a car," Harrigan said, taking out a small notepad. "1962 Plymouth Valiant. Pale blue. Sound familiar?"

"It does," he said. "That'd be Gina's."

The car, Harrigan explained, had been found about twenty yards off the road, wedged between a couple of sturdy trees, at the edge of a pine grove. "The whole thing was buckled like it was trying to go right through them."

"Jesus," Red gasped. "How the hell does someone survive that, much less walk away?"

"Most wouldn't," Harrigan shrugged. "Apparently there was a. . . ." He paused to look at his notepad. "There was an adult male," he continued, "some distance from the car. Likely by way of the windshield and a glance off one of the trees."

Red felt a chill run from his legs to his neck. "They give you a name?"

Harrigan shook his head, and right away the image of Frankie came to mind.

"Did they say if he was passenger or the driver?"

Harrigan shook his head again. "You'll have to call the police in Rockview for more details. At any rate, Gina's the one they want to talk to."

Red settled back against the grill of his truck, a wave of nausea sweeping over him. He looked over to Linda. She was close to the glass, with her hand cupped over her forehead, shielding it from the glare of the neon beer sign above her.

Harrigan took out a business card and turned it over. "Here's the phone number at the Rockview station," he said. "I guess they pulled the registration from the wreck, still listing you as the owner." He handed Red the card. "That's how they knew to call you."

Red took the card and looked at the name, the same name as the voice on his answering machine. Brody. Of course he'd call the guy, even though he had nothing to offer that would be worth a damn. The last phone number he'd had of Gina's had been disconnected months ago. And anyway, it's not like he even knew where the hell she might be living at any given moment.

Red thanked Harrigan. Once he was gone. Red gave Linda a wave of his hand and watched as she pulled back from the window and disappeared from sight, only to emerge a few moments later coming through the front door of the tavern. Before the door could even swing closed behind her, she called out. Red reached back to steady himself on his truck as his legs trembled under the weight of his body. Linda rushed over to him, putting her arms around him, her body warm and sweet against his.

"Gina had an accident with the car," he said. "Wrapped it around a tree somewhere in Idaho."

"Damn it! Is she—"

"No," Red interrupted. "Nowhere to be found, at least not by the time the cops got on the scene. There was a passenger, though." Red felt the words catch in his throat. "Some guy."

Linda pulled back, looked at him square in the eyes, and when he shook his head she whispered, "Oh, Red." She fell against him again, and they stood like that for a little while, the two of them shoulder to shoulder, Linda rubbing her hand over his arm while he ran a million possibilities of what he could or should do about any of it.

It was six months or so after she and Frankie had been at the house. Gina was at other end of the line, sobbing her eyes out after she'd managed to somehow back into the glass storefront of some mom-and-pop grocery outside Portland.

"I'll pay you back," she promised, again. "I'll come home and get a job and pay rent—whatever you want."

"What about Frankie?" Red asked her.

She puffed air into the phone, like she was blowing out a candle. "Don't get me started on Frankie," she said. Then, "Can you just talk to the guy at the store?" There was a scuffling noise, then the sound of someone clearing their throat.

"She's upset but she's okay." The man spoke with some effort, mumbling through what was likely mostly gums and few teeth. "I think she just got confused with the shifting and all. Shit happens." Red felt sorry for him. This poor fellow should've been living the rest of his days on a porch-rocker listening to birds, not hanging plywood over a busted-out picture window thanks to a damn girl who was probably six beers into her day.

Red wrote down the store owner's address and promised to send him a check first thing, then asked him to put Gina back on the phone.

"I'm so done with it all," she cried. "Running. Begging for money to buy food. The people."

"What people?"

"Just..." She sniffed into the phone. "Fake people. Say one thing then do the opposite."

Red knew about this sort of thing, but held his tongue. "You can come home if you want," he told her. "Sleep in your own bed. I think I saw a sign in the window at the laundromat, looking for someone for the night shift. That could work."

She sniffed again. "It could. Maybe."

Maybe. There it was, the seed of another bait and switch.

"The car still good for the road?" he asked.

"It's fine."

"Well then, you square things away there and give me a call when you think you'll be heading back home." Red tried to measure his words, making it sound like things were settled.

"Yeah, okay," she said. "I'll call you tomorrow."

The call, of course, didn't come. Red dropped the check in the mail anyway and by the time it was over, it had cost him six hundred bucks and a week of the worst sleep he'd had since Gretchen's death.

"So, what's next?" Linda asked.

"Well, I'll give that fellow in Rockview a call when I get home," Red said, the jagged edge of anxious all over his voice. "If it'll make you happy."

"What's that supposed to mean?" she said.

"Christ, I know. I'm just breaking into a hundred different pieces on this."

"I'll tell you what," Linda said. "I'll follow you home and by the time we get there, maybe you'll have a plan that's less about making me happy and more about making you whole."

Red opened the front door, and was immediately gripped by a certain thickness in the air, what he assumed must be the remnants of the morning's overcooked coffee and last night's fried steak and onions, smells he wouldn't have given a moment's notice to if he wasn't with Linda. He went into the kitchen, turned on the light and pushed open the window. Then he walked into the living room and opened the roll top desk. In one corner, there was a stack of papers, all about or from Gina—envelopes from the state, the DMV, the Department of Social and Health—the kinds of things that spoke to everything she continued to neglect and deflect. There were postcards from random places, from Seattle to Portland to Walla Walla, and a few letters, which he'd read more than once. The most recent piece was from about a year ago, a photo postcard of Spokane Falls, with a note saying that she was in Idaho, that she was okay, but she needed money. There was no mention of Frankie or anyone else. Red had gone ahead and sent a money order using the address she'd written down, though he couldn't remember how much it had been for. The town was Rockview, Idaho. and it surprised Red that he hadn't remembered this earlier.

"Here's something," he said, holding the postcard up.

Linda came over and took the card from him, held it close to her face. "It's almost a year old," she said. "What do you think the chances are that she's still at that address?"

"I wouldn't take any bets," Red said, taking the postcard back. He went back to the kitchen and took the hand piece from the wall phone and dialed out the number Harrigan had given him. On the third ring, it picked up.

"Deputy Brody."

Red cleared his throat. "My name's Red Miller," he stammered.

"From out in Ash Falls. I'm Gina—Gina Miller's father."

"Ah yes, Mr. Miller." The man cleared his throat as well, and there was the sound of papers shuffling.

"I think you've been trying to reach me," Red continued.

"Indeed, I have. Thank you for calling." He paused. "I assume you talked with the officer I called earlier?"

"Yes, sir."

"And he filled you in on the details as we have?"

"He did, but he didn't seem to have a whole lot."

"Right." He paused again. The sound of a drawer opening and closing. "The first thing I need to know is whether or not you've heard from your daughter in the last forty-eight hours."

"I haven't," Red said. "I don't have the slightest clue where she is."

"I see. So, you don't have any sort of contact info on her? A recent local address, or a phone number?"

Red looked at picture of the waterfall, then turned the postcard over and looked at the address.

"I'm afraid I don't," he heard himself say. "My daughter and me...we don't talk a lot."

"I see," Brody said. "Well, I'm sorry to hear that." He let out a sigh, then continued. "Our hope of course is that she's all right. And her little one, too."

"I'm sorry," Red said, looking over at Linda. "Little one?" Her eyes widened.

There was a long pause on the other end of the line, and for a moment Red wondered if perhaps the line had been disconnected.

"Yes, sir," Brody finally said. "I don't want to alarm you, Mr. Miller, but that's actually a greater concern of ours. You see..." He went silent, and Red could just make out the sound of his breathing. "The rear of the car," Brody resumed. "The back seat. There was a good bit of blood there...Of course, it doesn't necessarily mean the worst, but with neither Gina nor the boy..."

There came a sudden swell of dizziness. Red rested a hand against the side table to steady himself. "You're telling me she's got a son? And they're both missing?"

"I'm afraid so. You weren't aware she had a child?"

"Jesus, no," Red snapped. "I told you, me and her don't talk a lot."

"Well, sir, I'm sorry you're getting caught up this way." Brody went on. "I'm afraid she's been something of a blip on our radar out here for some time. Nothing too serious, up to now." The sound of his throat clearing again. "But we do know Gina."

"Yet you don't know where she's living?" Red asked.

"Not at the moment, no," Brody replied. "I checked in with the usual folks, but so far we've been more or less shooting in the dark. I hoped you might be able to point us in a direction we haven't tried yet."

"I'm sorry," Red said. "I wish I could tell you more." His mind went back to the passenger in the car, and he asked Brody if he could tell him anything more there.

"We're still waiting for confirmation on the ID of the deceased," Brody answered. "We don't think he's a local boy, though."

Red looked over at Linda, who had pulled the high-backed chair from the living room, sitting forward with her elbows on her knees. It was getting dark, and she wasn't much more than a shadow, but Red could still see her watching him.

"This boy of hers," Red said into the phone, almost a whisper. "How old would you say he is?"

"Noah?" the officer said. "I'd say he's about two, now."

Noah. Two years, and not a single word from her about a

kid. Outside a breeze picked up, lazy, the leaves on the plum tree fluttering like feathers. It wouldn't be long before it would be bursting with fruit, weighing the branches down and dropping onto the grass, all the plums he never bothered to pick. The yellow jackets would be everywhere.

"Well, sir," Brody sighed into the phone, "I appreciate the call back. We'll take it from here, and if I come across anything further, I'll let you know."

"Thank you," Red replied, the words spilling out like a mistake. He hung onto the phone, though, listening to the sound of the deputy breathing on the other end, not knowing what more he was supposed to say.

"And if you could do the same," Brody said finally.

"Of course," Red answered, as if waking from a deep sleep. "If I hear from her." He hung up the phone. Linda stood up and walked into the light of the kitchen. She held her hands together against her chest, as if in prayer.

# 5

The smell of onions hit first—sharp, clean, a little wet. Red's eyes watered as he worked the knife, slicing the half-moons into neat lines across the cutting board. The counter beside him was already crowded: canned tomatoes, a bottle of olive oil, the sauce pot Linda had pulled from the cabinet. Beside him, Linda worked the can opener around a dented can of sauce, the rhythmic click a counterpoint to the chopping of the knife.

"You didn't tell me what the sheriff said," she said, tipping the sauce into the pot.

"Wasn't much to tell beyond what you heard me say." Red reached into an open loaf of bread and took out a slice, laying it next to the onions. "She's got a little boy. You heard that."

"I did." Linda turned the dial on the stovetop burner. "How do you feel about that?"

"It feels strange, that's for sure," he said. "Certainly raises the stakes a bit." He decided to hold onto the detail about the blood.

"And he doesn't know where she might be?" she asked, stirring the pot. The scent of tomato began to fill the small kitchen. "Or if she's okay?"

Red reached for another onion, wiping at his eyes with his

sleeve. "He doesn't know any more than I do."

Linda reached past him and took a hand towel from the hook and dabbed at his face. "It doesn't have to be this bad, you know."

Red paused, the knife hovering over the wood block. "Are you talking about the onions or something else?"

Linda swatted the towel at him. "Maybe both." She smiled. "Tell me again where all this happened?"

"Idaho," he answered. "Someplace up the panhandle."

The sauce began to bubble. Linda turned down the heat, then looked over at Red. "And you're not going to tell me what else he said?"

He let the knife rest. "Linda, I told you. They found the car wedged into some trees, and a guy dead on the ground. They think Gina was driving but they don't know for sure. It's all a guessing game right now and I'm not getting worked up about it until there's something real." He tried to keep his tone measured.

She studied him for a moment longer, then nodded, though he could see she didn't buy it. "All right. I'll drop it." She moved past him to the cupboard to get some salt, brushing his shoulder lightly. The touch was easy, familiar. The smell of simmering sauce filled the silence. Red kept his head down, slicing, as though the motion itself could keep him from saying more.

They lay in bed with the window cracked open, a cool draft slipping through the curtains and stirring the faint smell of pine from outside. Linda sat up with a paperback open on her lap, glasses low on her nose. Red lay flat beside her, hands folded across his chest, staring at the ceiling as if piecing together a map in his mind.

"You're still thinking about her," Linda said without looking up from her book.

"I'm thinking about sleeping," Red said.

She turned a page. "You'd think all that chopping and crying would've worn you out."

He gave a dry laugh. "Guess I'm not as easy to wear out as I used to be."

"Maybe you should take a day off from Molly's Fairlane. Sleep in for once."

"I'd probably just lay around waiting for the phone to ring."

"Well," she said, "you could clean out that hall closet. I could help you organize all those stacks of magazines in the spare bedroom."

Red turned his head toward her, a faint grin tugging at his mouth. "Says the gal who saves everything and then calls me a hoarder."

"That's fine," she answered. She smiled, then closed the book and set it on the nightstand. "If you don't want me seeing what magazines you have in that pile…"

Red huffed out a laugh and reached over to turn down the lamp. The room dimmed to a soft amber glow.

"Feels nice in here," Linda said. "Quiet."

"It's too quiet most nights," Red said. "House feels too big."

"That's because you don't really live in it."

"What's that supposed to mean?"

"Means you prefer to live around the edges. Avoid talking too much about what's in your head. About Gina. About Gretchen."

"That's not true," he said automatically.

Linda folded her glasses and set them on the nightstand atop the book. "I was looking at that photo wall earlier," she said. "Gina in that red jacket. Gretchen beside her. She sure was a cutie."

"Yeah," Red said. "She was. Never sat still long enough for

the camera, though. Me and Gretchen used to joke about that. Christ, that girl had energy."

Linda smiled faintly. "Takes after her daddy, maybe."

"Gretchen wasn't a perfect mother by any means, but she knew how to handle Gina. Knew how to channel all that wildness. I never did figure that part out. Tried to fill in after she was gone, but… most of the time I was just stomping through everything, trying not to break the China."

"Don't sell yourself short," Linda said softly. "You had heart."

Red turned toward her. "Yeah, well 'heart' didn't do the trick, did it?"

"Sometimes it's the only thing that keeps you showing up," she said. "That's worth something."

He looked away. The clock on the dresser ticked slow and heavy. Outside, a car passed, tires hissing over the pavement. The whole thing had been so messy, and somewhere in all that mess was the picture of their lives, but goddamn if Red could see it at the time. It was as if they'd been living in one of those paintings that a person has to stand across the room from just to have it make some kind of sense. Try as he might, Red could never get past the smeared colors, could never put his and Gina's lives together into something he could hang up and be proud of.

"You ever think maybe you should go?"

He frowned. "Go where?"

"Idaho."

He faced her now. "And what good would that do?"

"You might have better luck with the locals than the sheriff. You could find her. Her and Noah."

"And then what? Drag them back here, pretend none of it happened?"

"It's not about pretending. It's about trying."

He sighed. "You think she wants me to show up out of the blue?"

"Maybe it's not about what she wants," Linda said quietly. "Maybe it's about what you need."

He didn't answer. The room went still again.

Finally, she reached out, resting a hand on his arm. "All right," she said after a beat. "I'll leave it alone."

It was near two when he woke. The room was dim, the soft blue light from the streetlamp bleeding through the curtains. The bathroom door down the hall was ajar, a faint sliver of yellow reaching across the carpet.

Red sat on the edge of the bed, rubbing his face, and after a moment, got up, heading to the kitchen for a glass of water. The tap groaned as he filled the glass, the cold biting against his teeth when he drank. Outside the window, the street lay empty. Across the road, the neighbor's yard held an old swing set, rusted, one chain hanging loose. Red watched the swing, and the memory came easy. Gina at three years old, bare feet, curls flying, on the swing he'd built from a kit one summer afternoon. "Higher, daddy!" she shouted, Gretchen on the porch laughing and telling her to hold on.

Red rested a hand on the edge of the sink. Maybe Linda was right. Maybe he should go.

He stood there a while longer, staring out at that rusted swing swaying a little in the night breeze, and tried to remember the sound of Gina's laughter—sharp and bright, like something that still might find its way home.

The gray light came slow through the curtains, dull and cold, the kind that made the day feel older than it was. Red sat on the edge of the bed pulling on his socks, careful not to wake Linda. She'd rolled onto her stomach sometime in the night, one arm thrown across the empty side of the bed where he'd been.

He looked at her for a long moment, then stood and started gathering things from the dresser—shirt, jeans, the small brown suitcase that had already seen too many miles.

In the kitchen, he brewed a pot of coffee and waited for the percolator to finish its slow chug.

By the time Linda stirred awake and came down the hall, he'd already poured two mugs and set one on the table for her.

"You're up early," she said, tying her robe.

"Couldn't sleep."

She eyed the suitcase near the door. "So you're really going."

"Guess I am."

Linda crossed the room and stood in front of the photo wall, where Gina's childhood stared back in frozen flashes. Red came to stand beside her. He pointed at a photo of Gina in the snow, rolling a watermelon-sized ball over the ground, the image sharp and clear except for the soft blur that was Gina. "Christ, that girl never stopped moving."

"Like she was scared to," Linda said.

"Maybe so."

They stood a long time without speaking. The coffee steamed on the table behind them.

"You know where you're staying?" Linda asked finally.

Red shook his head. "I'll figure that out once I get there."

"Well, if it turns out that boy comes back with you," she said, turning toward him, "I could do some shopping. Pick up a few things at the Salvation Army. You've got that second bedroom. Could put a little bed in there if you had to."

"Linda." He took a breath, choosing his words. "There's a lot we don't know yet. We don't even know if he's—"

"Don't say it," she cut in gently, waving her hands as if to brush the thought away. "Let's just go in hoping for the best."

Red looked away, toward the living room. The house suddenly felt too small and fragile for what might be coming. He tried to picture Noah here—small hands grabbing at picture frames, a laugh echoing down the hall. For a brief second, he almost smiled. But then it slipped away as quick as it came.

"Well anyway," he said, his voice gruff. "Don't go buying a bunch of kiddie stuff till I get over there and find out what the hell's going on. For all we know, she could be halfway across the country by now."

Linda nodded, though her eyes stayed soft and worried. "I know. But still… maybe pack an extra picture of her. In case you need to show it around." She walked down the hallway to a lone photo on the wall across from the spare bedroom. It was the picture of Gina at sixteen, her hair pulled back, defiant smile half-formed. A small photo in a large frame.

"No—" Red began to say, but it was too late. Linda plucked the photo from the wall, then paused, taking her breath in sharp.

Behind the frame was a hole about the size of a softball.

"Oh," Linda said. "I guess this one's been doing double duty."

Red took the frame from her and slid the photo from the cardboard backing. "I've been meaning to patch that since forever," he said, tucking the picture into his shirt pocket.

Linda took the empty frame from his hands and returned it to the wall. "Out of sight, out of mind."

For the rest of the morning, they talked about anything that didn't circle back to Gina—old movies, car troubles, vacation spots neither of them would ever see. The words came slow and careful, but they were enough to steady him.

When it was time, he poured the last of the coffee down the sink, grabbed his keys, and stood by the door.

Linda came to him, straightened the collar on his shirt, and held him for a long time—longer than usual. When he tried to pull back, she held on tighter.

"Just one time," she whispered, "I'd sure like it if you waited long enough for me to let go first."

He smiled against her hair. "If I did that, I might be standing here all day."

When she finally released him, she rested a hand on his cheek. "Red Miller, sometimes I swear I'm still turning over new stones with you every day. What I wouldn't give to climb inside that mind of yours."

"You wouldn't sleep for months," he said. Then he picked up his suitcase and stepped out into the morning.

# 6

The grass was high again, almost too high for the reel mower. Red had meant to get to it earlier in the week, but every time he thought about dragging the mower out of the shed, something else got in the way. A phone call. A casserole dish dropped off by someone he barely knew, who didn't seem to want to stay. A stare from Gina that lasted just a little too long.

Now she was out there, eight years old and tearing barefoot through the yard with a feral kind of energy kids get when the air is thick with summer and there's nothing to hold them back. Her hair was wild and whipped behind her like a kite tail, and she wore one of Gretchen's old cotton blouses, buttoned all crooked and falling almost to her knees like a dress. She wasn't chasing anything. Just running. Circles. Sprints. Sudden stops as she'd hit an invisible wall, then—bam—she'd be off again. Red watched from the kitchen window, coffee in hand, though it had long since gone cold.

It had been three weeks, maybe four. It wasn't as if he was keeping track, not the way people seemed to expect him to. Marking dates were for doctor appointments and bill payments. Grief didn't give a damn what the calendar said.

Inside the house, everything still smelled faintly of Lysol and cigarettes. Gina had taken to sleeping on the couch, curled up with a stuffed dog that Gretchen had picked up a few years before, Red couldn't remember where. It was an ugly thing with coarse, green fur and pink ears, and a missing eye. As far as Red could tell, the dog hadn't really meant much to Gina before, but now she wouldn't let the thing leave her side.

Gina also spoke less than she used to, but when she did talk, her voice came sharp and fast, as if it had cut its way out of her throat. Once, when Red asked what she wanted to eat for breakfast, she grabbed the carton of milk and tipped it straight to her mouth, sending most of it sloshing down the front of her shirt. When he asked her what the hell that was all about, she just stood there, fists tight, daring him to make something of it.

She barreled past the tire swing, then she stopped in her tracks, looked to the sky and screamed—high and shrill and full of fury. Red flinched. Then she collapsed onto the ground with her arms flung wide, spread out like she was offering herself up to the clouds. She clutched at the grass and started pulling up tufts by the handful, flinging them into the air and letting them fall on her until she was nearly covered. Finally, she let her arms fall, and Red thought he could see her lips move, though he wasn't sure. Maybe she was just talking to herself. Maybe she was just talking to someone who wasn't there anymore.

Red was just past The Sleep Inn Motel and the River Road turnoff when a school bus pulled out onto the highway in front of him. There were a scattering of kids inside. It was July. It could be a summer school thing, he thought. Slow learners, or trouble-makers taking some of their precious vacation days to try and make up what they didn't do when everyone else did.

The bus slowed to a stop, its red sign jutting out, flashing lights winking at him. A couple of girls, barely teenagers, emerged from behind some salmonberry bushes on the shoulder and climbed aboard.

The idea of relocating himself and Gina all the way out to Ash Falls had been a suggestion by a foreman at the mill. It was an hour's drive east up into the North Cascades, but there was a smaller outfit up there, the guy said. Red could probably get on as a shift supervisor, with his experience and all. Gina would have room to run. "That town's full of kids like her," he said, a sentence Red was unsure whether he should take as a promise or a warning.

Red managed to get on at McKay Lumber with a promotion in rank and a small cut in pay, easy enough to withstand thanks to the modest price tags on several in-town bungalows that were listed for sale. He made an offer on one a couple blocks off of Main Street and moved in with Gina, mustering the best hopes he could.

For a while, things did pick up for them. She made a new friend, a girl whose name Red could never seem to remember. Gina would spread her homework out on the kitchen table while Red made them supper. There were funny stories she wanted to tell him, and on a few occasions, she asked him to read to her before bed, something she hadn't done before. She stopped blaming him for taking her away from her old life, to "the dark forest" as she called it. It seemed like everything would be okay after all.

But in time the edge of the leaves started to curl as she began to sink into her old ways, finding all new ways to disappear, to rise above, grab hold and push away. Pretty soon Red got a call from the school: "She refuses any reasonable instructions."

They sat on opposite sides of a giant desk—Red on one

side, the principal on the other, the wall behind him a clutter of framed degrees and certificates and photos of people who looked happy to be standing with one another. A slight man with serious eyes, the principal fussed with his necktie, a spread of marked-up papers in front of him. The teacher, a mousey-looking thing with chapped skin around her eyes, sat to his side, stock still, her hands buried in her lap.

"Her mother passed last year," Red explained. "Not that I'm using it as an excuse. You just got to be firm with her." He acknowledged that she wasn't easy, and he told them she'd always been that way. Always so eager to do whatever it was that popped into her head, then deal with the consequences later. "Her mother had a way with her," he went on, "better than I ever did." He was surprised and ashamed to feel his throat tightening when he said this. He had no desire to look soft in front of these people. He paused, caught his breath. "I wished I'd have paid closer attention."

"I sympathize with you, Mr. Miller, I really do." The principal smoothed his tie into place, his eyes relaxing some. Red could not remember the last time he'd worn a tie. "But the impulsivity and constant opposition and acting out..."

"She's quite impossible," the teacher interjected, her voice shaking. "She can't walk from one place to another without putting her hands on someone. And if I want her to finish any kind of work, I have to stand right behind her." She went on like that, firing a machine gun litany of offenses.

Finally, Red put his hand up. "Goddamn, is there anything she does well besides cause trouble?"

"Mr. Miller—" the teacher sputtered.

"She's damaged, I know that," Red continued. "Her mother drowned in the bath less than twenty feet away from her, for

Christ's sake. I know she's work. But from where I'm sitting, it's like you're all ready to give up on her."

The teacher drew a sharp breath in through her mouth, pressed her lips together. As if she was holding whatever else she wanted to say behind her teeth.

"We're not giving up on her, Mr. Miller," the principal said. He put his hands up like he was calming a rearing horse. "On the contrary. But the other students are starting to be affected. The current situation is unsustainable."

"You're right, it's unsustainable," Red replied.

"I'm glad you agree."

They sat in silence for a good moment, the teacher staring down at her hands, Red and the principal holding one another's gaze. Finally, Red blinked.

"I apologize," he said. "For getting riled up. You probably think I'm impossible, too."

"Parenting can be tough," the principal said.

In the end, the meeting concluded with a half-assed agreement that everyone would work harder, whatever that was supposed to look like. Red collected Gina to go home with him. The whole ride home, neither of them said a word. Red understood that the slightest suggestion on his part would unleash a torrent from her.

It wasn't until they pulled into the driveway that she spoke up.

"They want to control me," she said, her voice low and stretched tight.

"Who does?" Red asked.

"Everyone at that stupid school." She glared out the window, at the split rail fence that ran from their house, down the grassy slope to the edge of the asphalt road. "But I won't let them."

"Believe me, honey, I know," Red answered. "We all know."

The sun had reached the point in its descent where his visor could finally block its glare. It would be another four hours or so until he got himself to Spokane, and then another hour or so before he could manage to find this place called Rockview. Red had never been fond of this drive, the long climb over the pass into the eastern side of the mountains. But there was no other way, and he told himself that at least he had the summer clock to shepherd him. Another few months and it'd be all snow, darkness and the slow crawl of traffic most of the way. Small blessings.

The truck had cooperated with him, all the way to the summit. A breakdown had been his one worry, at least as far as the drive. It was strange how that concern always seemed to be with him. While he could take care of someone else's rig in a single afternoon, discover what was responsible for a certain rattle or knock, then watch the owner pull out from his driveway with the engine purring like a kitten, when it came to his own pickup, he never could seem to find the time and energy to do what needed to be done.

It had been under the watchful eye and firm thumb of his father that Red had learned to dismantle and clean a carburetor before he even learned how to drive. In time, he could rebuild an entire engine if he had to. The removal and deconstruction, rebuilding and replacement, filled him with a satisfaction that just didn't happen with anything else. It was within the process of repair that a fire was stoked inside him. Under the open hood and warmth of a trouble light, he could work miracles.

As the truck dipped down the other side of the mountain, Red watched the needle on the fuel gauge jump from one side to the other, before finally settling down just below a quarter tank. He eyeballed the highway ahead of him, watching for a gas station somewhere out there.

Just as he was beginning to measure out how far he might have to walk with an empty gas can, he came upon a little Gas n' Go. The price per gallon was through the roof, but he'd expected as much. He pulled up to the first pump and climbed out of the cab. A cool breeze washed up from the south clearing, accompanied by the soothing whisper of the Skykomish River as it rolled down the mountain.

At the far edge of the lot there was a thick wall of blackberry bushes. A couple of kids crouched on their haunches, peering into the brambles. At first, Red thought they might be picking berries, but it was too early for fruit, even east of the mountains.

A woman came out through the doors of the store and paused, then scanned the lot before finally laying eyes on the kids. One of the kids turned and shouted to her, "There's kittens, Mom!" Sure enough, a little black thing darted out from the underbrush, scurried between the kids, and then disappeared into the brambles again.

"For god's sake don't touch 'em," the woman called. "They're probably riddled with fleas and ringworm."

They used to have a gray tabby named Wilfred that they'd gotten as a kitten right after Gina was born. Even though the cat had been Gretchen's idea, it was Red who gave him all the ear scratches and table scraps. After Gretchen's death, it was Wilfred's warmth and the hum of his purring that acted as a kind of respite at night, the cat in his lap while Red watched the late show. By the time Gina hit her teen years and her business of running away and making herself known to the local police kicked in, Wilfred had long since passed. Yet no matter how lonely the chair they once shared seemed, Red just couldn't bring himself to take on another responsibility, whether it was a cat or anything else.

"Abby already touched 'em." The younger of the two kids, a boy of probably about seven, stood up. He was a redhead, with hair as unruly and orange as Red's had been at his age. The boy took a couple steps toward his mother, pointing behind himself at the girl. "There's four of 'em and she touched three."

"I did not!" The girl protested.

The mother threw her head back with a groan. She walked over to the kids and took the girl by the wrist and marched her to the side of the building, to an open door that Red could only assume was the toilet.

At the base of the bushes, a smattering of black and white fur balls emerged, and then a larger cat, black with a chest full of white. The boy turned back and watched them, bouncing up and down on his toes.

Red held the nozzle and let the gauge creep to an even ten bucks. By this time, the kittens were all out from under the bushes and tumbling around in a grassy patch that ran along the gravel bed. The boy stood at some distance from them now, stealing glances at the restroom door where his sister, considering how long they'd been in there, was most likely getting a full disinfection from their mother.

Red put the nozzle back into the pump, then walked over to the boy. "They sure are something," he said.

The boy turned and smiled at him, an empty space where a front tooth had been. "I wish we could take 'em," he said. "But my mom would say no."

"I imagine she would," Red said. "Moms, they have to be practical."

"Practically always," the boy said seriously.

The mama cat had wandered over to the trash bin and was sniffing around a discarded paper sack that hadn't made it inside.

"I wonder if she would know if someone took one." The boy swayed a bit on his feet, as if he was contemplating getting a few steps closer. The laces of one of his sneakers fell loosely over the ground. He was all dirty knees and elbows, and in need of a good haircut. Then again, summer allowed for less tidiness.

The door to the restroom swung open and mother and daughter emerged back into the sunlight. The girl's face was pink, her eyes puffy and red as if she'd been crying.

"She might notice," Red said to the boy. "If one of her babies were gone."

"And then she would be sad."

"I suppose she would be," Red said.

"Jody." The woman called over. "We're leaving."

The boy snapped to attention, gave the cats one final look before saying, "Bye kitties," and running off with that shoelace slapping to a dust-covered Pinto parked against a low stack of railroad ties at the far end of the lot.

Red went inside the shop and laid a ten spot on the counter, then turned and scanned the few rows of groceries and snack foods and camping supplies that ran back to the wall of beer coolers.

"You got any pet food here?" he asked. "Cat food?"

"Let me guess. For the stray outside," the woman behind the counter said. She had on a long-sleeved T-shirt with a picture of a howling wolf on it, a snake of salt and pepper braided and draped over her shoulder, just coming to set there on her breast.

"There's little ones," Red said.

"Fat little ones," she laughed. "At least once a day someone picks up something to feed 'em with. Tuna. One of these hot dogs. Cheese. Those things eat better than I do."

Red grabbed three cans of sardines, and went outside and

laid them out on the grass. The kittens mewed and swarmed over the food, the mother following close behind. If they were over-fed, that wouldn't be the worst thing. And while he considered for a short minute that he might scoop one of them up to take with him, the last thing he needed was a kitten under his wing. As it stood, he might end up with a hell of a lot more to take care of than a pet.

# 7

He hit the Idaho border in the late afternoon. Leaving the interstate, he took 95 north, passing through towns that were nothing more than weathered mercantiles and a few clapboard houses. The sun had almost set behind him, a long shadow dragging over the sage like a giant, black paintbrush. A water tower announced that he would be coming into Rockview at the next exit.

By now, Red could feel his body turning on him, the muscles in his back and neck pushing hard from the drive. The thought of stretching out on a bed actually made his eyes well up. There would be a motel in town, he assumed, and surely a place to get a decent bite to eat. He'd get some rest and plan his next move with his head on a pillow.

He stopped at a burger joint, one of those drive-in stands where teenagers sat in cars and pickups with the doors wide open and shared their music with the world. The girl behind the counter was kind enough to point him to a motel. "It's called The Top Hat," she said. "I don't think it's the cheapest one in town, but they got a pool and they keep it clean."

The Top Hat was a single-story building, opposite an old craftsman-type house with a high signpost reading French and Sons Funeral Home. The motel was laid out in a horseshoe configuration with the pool in the middle. There were lights on the deck with the blue glow hovering over the water and reflecting against the cinderblock walls.

Red took the last bite of his burger and climbed out of the pickup. As he pulled open the glass door to go inside the motel office, a young, mustached guy with his hair tied up in a ponytail looked up at him from the desk.

"Evening."

"Evening," Red replied.

"Looking for a room?"

"If you got one."

The kid got up, flipped open a book. "How many nights?" His mustache brushed against his lips when he talked, and Red thought it was the type of thing that was new to him, the soft downy hair that hadn't had years of being shaven and regrown. It was a mustache wished for, probably monitored daily in a hand-held mirror at home.

"Well, I'm not sure," Red answered.

"That's fine," the kid said. "Just let us know by noon."

Red gave the kid his credit card and signed a piece of paper, making note of the ice maker and vending machines in the lobby. Before he left to go to his room, he took the postcard from his pocket. "I was wondering if you could tell me where this place is," he said, laying the card on the counter and pressing his thumb on the address. The kid leaned in to read it, then looked up at Red. His eyebrows raised in an arch as if Red might be putting something over on him.

"You know somebody there?"

"I hope so. I'm looking for my daughter, Gina Miller." He felt a surprising pinch in his stomach; the simple act of saying her name could still do what it once did.

"Your daughter?"

"And my grandson," Red added. Again, the stomach pinch.

The clerk shook his head. "I don't hang there, but I can draw you a map. It's a few miles from here." He slid open a drawer and fished out a pen. "It's a nasty, shitty place, no offense. Just last spring a dude got stabbed in the head in the parking lot. Walked halfway down the street with this little pocketknife sticking up like a horn or some shit before someone finally stopped to help him."

"Jesus," Red gasped. He had seen his share of split lips and cut knuckles, but the thought of a two-year-old living in the middle of something like that gripped his heart like a vice.

"I don't mean to spook you, but I hope to hell you ain't thinking of going by there tonight."

"I was. But it sounds like I'd be better off waiting till daylight."

The kid looked at Red as if he was crazy to even consider going there at all. He grabbed a sheet of paper from the desk and scratched out a mural of lines and boxes and took Red through the town of Rockview, from The Top Hat to the downtown core where he said there was a Rexall drugstore and a tractor dealership next to a domed building with flags out front. He narrated the whole journey as if he were the one driving, showing Red the highlights of the town he had presumably grown up in. There was a little store that used to be a hobby shop that now sold sewing machines. The library was next to his mother's workplace; there was a diner called The Blue Saucer. He told Red that after he drove through all of that, there would be a long stretch of road that snaked its way through a spread of land built up with a bunch of greenhouses, and then some distance past that he would finally see the apartment complex he was looking for. It might be dirty white or maybe it was green now, but at any rate, Red would know it by the ugliness of it all. "It's the kind of place where you know shit is either going down or is about to."

Red walked past a row of rooms, the clicking light of television sets filtering through drawn shades. The numbers on the doors ticked upward, and next to the spot where his room was, a glow of red light spilled out into the walkway. As he got closer, he could see that the light was coming from a string of chili pepper lights that someone had strung from the window. A banner of paper decorations sagged along the eaves—sombreros and cocktail glasses.

"Jesus," he thought. "There better not be a party, cause I sure as hell ain't in the mood."

Red let himself into his room and switched on the light. The space was not much to look at, but it was tidy. The bed was covered in a simple blue spread, nothing quilted or fringed. There was a single desk against the wall that held a television set. There were a couple of matching paintings above the desk, scenes of a train coming out of the mountains. Smoke from the stacks bled into the sky, a haze erasing the mountains. Red wasn't an artist, but he knew a spoiled view when he saw one.

He set out his clothes for the next day and walked back down to the office to use the payphone. The kid was in a small lobby area now, stretched out on a well-worn sofa watching a black and white movie on a console TV. A man on a horse was laboring up a mountain trail—maybe Robert Mitchum, but Red couldn't be sure.

He picked up the phone and dialed the operator, giving them Linda's number, then said what he always said when there was no intention of either of them paying the toll: "Collect call from George." Of course she would be expecting it, not minding that there would be no conversation—it was enough simply to know that he'd made it safely. All the same, the charade always carried with it such a weight of disappointment, the distant voice on the other end, the expectant "hello?" upon answering, and then nothing more. And even though this was what they did to save a few dollars, even though he could see her knowing grin and maybe a roll of the eyes when she heard the name, to hear her say, "I'm sorry, I can't accept the charges," would pull on him, as if he was standing on the opposite side of a great river as she was walking away, unable to hear his call over the roar of the rapids. As if she did not know him at all.

There was a time when Red thought that every telephone operator in the state of Washington and beyond must have known him and Gina from all the collect calls she made to him from the road.

"I just wanted to let you know I'm fine," she'd say to him.

"Okay, then," he'd respond. "If you want me to buy a bus ticket from wherever you are—

"Maybe in a few days," she'd say, or just, "No, Dad."

A little negotiation might follow, then a short drive by Red to Western Union to send a few dollars her way so she could eat, or buy gas for somebody who'd been driving her around. In his gut Red knew she was playing him like a deck of cards, but it was a cheap price to pay for a little peace of mind just to know that she was alive.

He emptied his medicine bag beside the bathroom sink.

Linda had packed it better than he'd have done—razor, toothbrush and paste, some aspirin and Alka-Seltzer. A few Band-Aids. He laid it all out in a kind of inventory, then stretched himself out on the bed, staring up, his eyes searching the curious topography of the popcorn ceiling. The sound of trumpets rose from next door, but softly. Mariachi, maybe.

Before he drifted off to sleep, Red found himself wondering about those kittens, and what they might be doing right then.

He woke to the sun breaking through the curtains and the sound of squealing and slapping on water. The clock read nine o'clock, and Red couldn't believe that it was possible to have slept so long, but there it was staring right back at him.

He dragged himself from the bed and got dressed, slipped on his trucker's cap, and walked down to the lobby to get himself a cup of weak motel coffee before heading out to try and find Gina's place. He wasn't gone ten minutes when he came back to see the door to his room blocked by the housekeeping cart.

"You gotta be quick on your toes around here," he heard a voice say. Behind him, near the swimming pool, a woman sat in a plastic lounger under the shade of a wide, orange umbrella. She wore a John Deere cap too big for her head, and a red-striped bathing suit with denim cutoff shorts over the bottom half. A short glass of something fruity sat on an adjacent table. "These gals are nothing if not efficient," she said, picking up a cigarette and taking a drag.

Red walked through the wrought iron enclosure into the pool area. The woman reached into a cooler and held up a quart carton.

"I'm happy to share if you're thirsty."

"Got anything with a little potency in there?"

"Don't you think it's a little early?"

Red laughed. "There was a time when I might have challenged that," he said. "Anyway, this coffee here will likely do more damage than anything else."

Two kids, brown-skinned and chattering in Spanish, cycled from the diving board to the ladder and back again. Red went over and sat on a folding chair.

"I'm Sadie," the woman said. "That's my dad Morris over there." She glanced toward a figure in the pool, an old man wrapped in what looked like a padded life preserver. His thin, white hair stood up like a baby chick's tuft as he moved slowly through the water, bobbing up and down. "We're your neighbors."

Red looked over at Sadie. It was hard to tell how old she was, but considering Morris' advanced age, Red figured she probably clocked in at forty-something.

"I'm Red. Those aren't your kids over there, are they?"

"God no," she said, then held up her hand. "Oh shit, I didn't mean that the way it probably sounded. Like, because they're Mexican or anything. I honestly don't know who their parents are. They show up almost every day and stay for about an hour or so. I haven't seen anyone looking after them so I'm guessing they're just local kids who slip through the gate when they can."

One of the boys ran to the end of the diving board and launched himself into the air, hitting the water and sending a wave up onto the pool deck. Morris took a light spray but did little more than wince.

"How long are you here for?" Sadie asked.

"A couple days. Maybe more," Red said. "Depends on a few things."

Sadie sat up and swung her legs over to the side of her chair, leaning in toward Red. "I'm gonna ask you something, Red," she said, her voice low. "A favor, if you don't mind."

Red reached up and scratched his head under his cap. He wasn't sure there was room for anything else on his plate. "I'll hear you out," he said. "But I can't promise anything."

"So, I know this is going to sound crazy," she said. "And before you judge me for what I'm doing I want you to know that I have come to believe that even though honesty is usually the best policy, as folks say, sometimes it's okay to lie now and then. You know? If it's for the right reason, I mean."

Red took pains to make sure that his expression gave her nothing to go on.

"Do you agree with that?" she asked. "That there are times when, in fact, lying is the best policy?"

Gina had disappeared for a few days, and Red spotted her at a park, standing among some other teenagers. He'd called out to her from the fence a good two or three times, but she didn't so much as throw a glance in his direction. A few of the other kids looked his way, so he knew she had heard him. "I'm going in the hospital in the next few days," he hollered. "I just thought you should know." It wasn't true, of course. A lie called out in desperation. Gina broke from the group and came over to him and, after a few questions, agreed to go home with him. He milked the lie for a few days, telling her he was going in for a few tests but going for steak and eggs at a diner outside town instead. At the end of it all, the "doctors" had cleared him and the trail of lies in this instance managed to reset things—at least until the next disagreement sent her off into the night.

"Lying," Red answered. "Yeah, I know a thing or two about that."

"Okay, then." Sadie took a drink from her glass. "So, you probably noticed the lights outside last night. And the music. I try to keep it down 'cause I know these walls ain't the thickest."

Red nodded.

"Anyway, you should know that my dad is kind of at the tail end of things up here, if you get what I mean," she said, tapping her forehead. "He can still do the basics—feed himself, toilet, carry on a simple conversation, more or less. But he's not always aware of what's up or what's down from one minute to the next. And the thing is, right now, he's under the impression that we're having a nice little vacation in Tijuana." Sadie stared down into her glass, swirling the liquid in gentle circles. She seemed to be replaying the story in her head, silently checking the boxes of what was right and what was forgivable. "And if it's all the same to you," she said, "I'd like to keep it that way."

One of the boys climbed out of the water and called to the other one. The slick rattle of Spanish suddenly felt like a script, as if pre-planned.

"Mexico, huh?" Red looked around him. The morning sun, already uncomfortable against his back. The pool, with its brown-skinned players. The half-hearted attempt at decor and music. He could see it working on a four-year-old.

"Him and my mom always talked about taking us kids to Tijuana someday, but for one reason or another it just never happened. Money, maybe. Work. Anyway, by the time mom passed away, his mind was already slipping, and I sure as hell didn't have the funds to make it happen. My brothers are useless in that way. Always have been."

"How many you got?" Red asked. "Brothers."

She held up two fingers in a V. "I'm the baby by several years and we're not close, so I don't really see them. They sure as hell don't take the time to see him more than one every few months. They probably don't even know he's been checked out of the home." Morris was coming up the steps now, out of the water. He walked over to a lounge chair draped with a long, orange-striped towel, and laid down.

"Dad," Sadie called out. "This is Red. Red, this is Morris."

"*Buenos Días*," Morris called over, raising an arm over his head.

"*Buenos Días*," Red sent back.

"Red's from the US," Sadie said, giving Red a side glance. "What city again?"

"Ash Falls," Red said. "About an hour or so from Seattle. Up in the mountains."

"I know it," Morris said.

"We lived in Monroe for about ten years. We're in Tacoma now. Isn't that right, Dad?"

"Tacoma," he repeated.

"It's a long way from Tacoma to Tijuana." Red said. He peeked at his watch then stood up, fanned himself with his cap. "I hate to cut this short, amigos, but I'm afraid I have some business to take care of. Depending on how things unfold, I may or may not return with company in tow."

"Not my business," Sadie said, holding up her hands.

"I don't mind the curiosity," he assured her. "I was just thinking I'd better hit the road before I change my mind about the whole thing." He turned to Morris. "*Adios*, Señor Morris." The old man raised his arm again in a kind of clumsy salute.

Red lowered both windows in the pickup in hopes of letting a bit of air flow through before climbing inside. Whatever breeze there was, it was a whisper at best. He could feel his scalp begin to itch and his body sweat under his clothes. If he had to guess he'd say the temperature was already pushing eighty.

Taking out the rudimentary map the kid in the motel had made, he ran his finger along the scrawled lines, scanning the roadway in both directions to get himself acclimated. There was a towering A&P sign down the way, the red letters coming and going as it rotated on its post. That was the direction he'd be headed. North, toward downtown, according to the map.

He climbed inside the pickup and fired up the engine, then steered his rig out into the open lot. Across the street sat a car, alone against the curb. From what Red could tell it was an El Camino, 1964 or so, he figured. He never really understood the logic of trying to cobble a pickup truck with a sedan, but he sure appreciated the effort. It looked to Red like there was somebody in the driver's seat, but it was too far away to make out any details.

"What a pretty thing you are," he said to himself. "I sure as hell wouldn't leave you parked on the side of the street."

He waited for a clear gap in the passing traffic then punched the gas, lurching out onto the main road. He opened her up and the air thundered in, thankfully cooling the cab. After a slow turn of the radio dial, he was able to land on a halfway decent western station to lift him out of his rut. A good dose of George Jones, he'd discovered years earlier, could talk most any man from the ledge.

Downtown Rockview was a tour of churches, taverns and weathered storefronts, many of them either still closed for the morning or simply vacant, with "for rent" signs in place of drapes. There were shops named for people, first or last names, or simply initials. Lisa's Consignment. Meyer Hardware. JW and Sons. Cars clustered in the parking lot of The Blue Saucer, and the few people wandering the sidewalks carried themselves as if they'd been there all night, as if the light of day was a confusing and inconvenient thing.

Red passed through town, and, as the map indicated, he turned right at the bank, where he continued on a rough and poorly maintained drive, past a smattering of auto repair and farm equipment shops, to where the pavement snaked off into gravel drives, mobile home enclaves, the occasional lonely farmhouse, and cracker box houses set back amid knee-high grass and sickly oaks.

A stand of homes bled off the main roadway, ranches and bungalows ringed with low chain-link fences and unkempt lawns, wheaty and dry. And at the end of the drive, separated by barbed wire from a field of what looked to Red like corn stalks, was a single, broad boxlike building. It was pale blue and looked recently painted.

"It's the kind of place where you know shit is either going down or is about to."

He pulled into the parking lot, a rut and oil-spotted spread that he navigated like it was a test. At the edge of the building sat an abandoned, rust-streaked swing set, honeysuckle vines already creeping up the frame.

Red brought his truck to a stop in an open stall near the main stairwell, and he could sense that there were more people here than the number of cars indicated. Sheets for drapes waved through open windows, and from somewhere, the noise of kids echoed forth, laughing and screaming in play.

Red climbed from the cab and double checked the apartment number on the envelope before heading up to the second floor. The exterior walkway extended from one end of the building to the other, behind a long cage of curled wrought iron railing. The odor of cigarettes filled the air, accompanied by the scatter of discarded butts, crushed filters like gauzy insects on the concrete. He tracked the numbers as he walked, peel and stick decals tacked to the doors like you might put on a mailbox or a filing cabinet. At the far end, 228 stared back at him.

He gave the door a good rap with his knuckles, his heart picking up. When there was no immediate response, he knocked again, then stepped back and waited for whoever might open the door.

At last, he heard the drumbeat of footsteps coming and the door snapped open, though it was no more than a gap and a taut chain. A woman's face peered out at him. The face was too round and too dark to be Gina's. Red's whole body sank.

"I'm sorry to be a bother," he said. "I'm looking for my..." He felt himself press the brake. "For Gina. I'm looking for Gina Miller."

"She don't live here anymore." The woman looked down at the floor. "Three other people came here this past week already asking about her. I don't know her. I only been here a few months."

Three people? Besides the cops, whole else might be looking for her?

"Sounds like she's got a lot of friends," Red said. It was all he could think of.

"Friends that don't know where she is," the woman snapped. "Anyway," she added, "the manager lives downstairs in number 102. He might know something."

Red glanced behind the woman through the small opening in the door, not so much because he did not believe her but because he hoped to see a glimpse of where Gina had been, where she'd sat when she wrote out that postcard to him. There was a small, square table against the kitchen window, which looked like one of those built-in things. But then the woman said Bye, then and closed the door, the deadbolt sliding swiftly into place.

The manager took even longer to get to the door than the woman upstairs, but at least he swung it all the way open, standing in the entranceway looking like he'd just crawled out of bed, his hair twisted every which way. He was squat and barrel-bellied, and his strained yellowed undershirt just about—but not quite—stretched to his trousers.

"You bet your ass I remember her," he said. "Like you'd remember stepping on a hornets' nest."

He waved Red into his apartment. Even from the abbreviated view Red had gotten of Gina's old place, it was clear to him that this space was more or less a mirror copy—as far as the layout went, anyway. In the little galley kitchen was the same square tabletop aside a wooden bench, all of it crowded against the window. From down the hallway a small dog appeared from one of the bedrooms, sauntering out with a slow swing of his tail.

"I'm Charlie Polk and that there is Tito," the man said. "He ain't much of a watchdog." Tito's tail picked up at the sound of his own name.

"What is he, a kind of terrier?" Red asked.

"Kind of a pain in the ass is what he is." Charlie made a kissing sound at the dog. "Aren't you?" Again, the tail. "Can I get you something to drink?" he asked Red.

Red reached up and touched his face, which felt a bit warm. "I suppose something cold wouldn't be a bad idea," he said.

Charlie shuffled to the kitchen and came back with a couple of cans of Mr. Pibb. The two of them sat in opposite chairs in the living room, Red nearest the picture window that looked out into the parking lot.

"You from west of the mountains?" Charlie asked.

"How'd you guess?"

"You're pale as hell." He waved a hand over his face. "If you were from here, you'd be a few shades—"

"You said you remember her," Red interrupted. "Can you be more specific?"

Charlie sat up straight in his chair, like a schoolboy called out by his teacher. "Well yeah," he said. "First of all, there was all the fights. Hollering and cussing, doors slamming at all hours of the day and night. Her and that fella she had living with her. I told 'em more than once that I didn't like calling the cops on my tenants, but in their case, it was coming if they didn't knock it off. The guy tried to tell me it was all her, that she had a temper and he was only trying to talk sense into her." He took a drink from his Mr. Pibb, shook his head. "I told him I didn't give a rat's ass whose fault it was, but if I heard it again, either one or the both of 'em was gonna get their walking papers."

"What was the guy's name?" Red asked. "The boyfriend."

"Young guy. Hard to keep these things straight, what with so many people coming and going."

Red shifted in his seat. "How long would you say has it's been since she left here?"

"The boyfriend tore out of here one night I'd say about six months ago," he said. "Amid her screaming and hollering and pitching all his clothes to him from the balcony. Couple months later, I had to put her out. I hated to do it, but she hadn't paid a single dime of rent since he left."

"So round about April."

"Ezra." Charlie snapped his fingers.

Red cocked his head at him. "What's that?"

"Ezra was the kid's name. The boyfriend." Charlie broke into a broad smile, as if he'd solved a crime. Outside, a car thundered past, the notion of a muffler an afterthought.

"About her little boy," Red pressed. "Can you tell me anything about him?"

"To be honest, I hardly ever saw the boy. I'd catch sight of Gina now and then pushing one of them strollers. Walking down to the bus stop, I guess."

Red tried to bring the scene together in his mind. Gina had never shown anything close to a maternal bent, such as playing house or dressing up the many dolls Gretchen tried to push on her. The only real attention she gave to the things was the time she and a friend spent the better part of an afternoon scrawling what they said were 'tattoos' all over one of the dolls with a ballpoint pen. It wasn't anything nasty that he could see—stars and butterflies and hearts. But Gretchen was livid, sending the girl home and making Gina scrub the doll with Borax until everything was as faded as it was going to get. As for the friend, Red never saw her again, which was a real shame as Gina didn't have a line of kids waiting to play with her.

"I don't suppose she left a forwarding address," Red asked.

Charlie shook his head. "People come and go here all the time. Most times, I don't have the foggiest idea where their next stop is, especially if they're skipping out on rent or been put out by the sheriff. It's not like they're circling back to let me know where they're running off to."

Red looked out at the gravel parking lot—cars spotted with primer, gray patches on their fenders, one long sedan with plastic sheeting over the rear window. There was a lone tree against a low stretch of chain link, its branches smooth and naked but for a dozen or so curled, brown leaves.

"Well," Red sighed, "I guess I'll leave you to it." He stood up and brushed a feather of dog hair from his jeans.

"I'm sorry you had to come all the way out here for nothing,"

Charlie said. "Probably not what you hoped for."

"What I hoped for and what I expected were always pretty far apart," Red sighed.

As he went to leave, Charlie stopped him. "Hang on," he said. "I just remembered that that old boyfriend of hers came looking for her, sometime after I put her out. Said he wanted some of his stuff that he'd left behind but of course by then there was nothing. Anyway, he left his work number for me in case she ever came back, as if she would have the audacity to set foot here again."

Forty-five minutes and a half-cup of coffee later, Red found himself waiting at the base of a loading dock at Rockview Farm and Feed, breathing in the scent of hay dust and sweat. Young men moved around him, pushing weighted hand carts, lugging propane tanks, shouting questions at one another in the cavernous warehouse. An easy breeze discovered him as he stood there, cooling the space between his chin and his collar. He pulled back the top of his shirt to invite in more air.

"Mister Miller?"

A kid stood next to him, denim overalls bunched into mud-clotted boots. He was wearing a gray T-shirt, which brought out the tawny yellow of his hair, an unruly mop that stuck out like a carpet of straw.

Red extended his arm toward him. "That's me."

"I'm Ezra," the kid said, taking Red's hand. Though his grip was cool and clammy, it was a firm handshake.

"You sounded a hell of a lot older of the phone," Red said. "I don't mind saying you don't look old enough to drive much less to have been taking up with Gina."

The kid laughed. "I'm twenty-three, but yeah. I tend to lean toward older women if I'm being honest."

"Nothing inherently wrong with that, I guess." Red thought about how Ezra looked more or less like any other decent kid he'd ever seen. But what did he know? The truth was, you could never really tell what was happening inside people, the poisons that might be marking divots in their heads. Christ, he'd seen it growing up in his own house.

"Gina liked to have fun, for sure," Ezra said. "There was always something going on somewhere, but Noah—" He shook his head. "He was always under your feet, you know?"

"Inconvenient, I suppose."

"I don't mean it like that," Ezra said, his face flushing. "Yeah, he took some of the shine off. But he was just a baby. He didn't have a choice in any of it and that part made me feel pretty bad."

"But it didn't stop you from wanting what you wanted."

"I guess not," he said. "Gina would talk about finding someone to take him, and there were times when she acted like she was seriously thinking about it. Once she went down to the library and spent all day going through phonebooks from all over trying to track down Noah's dad, but nothing ever came of it."

"Frankie?" Red asked.

Ezra shrugged his shoulders. "I don't remember her even saying a name, just 'Noah's dad.'" He looked at Red, the edge of his mouth like a comma. "She even brought your name up once or twice...Gina and me really weren't together for very long, you know. Two, three months, maybe. Even so, it's a long story and to be honest Mr. Miller, it don't feel right me standing here bad-mouthing your daughter to you. I'd feel better just saying that things got really messed up between us and leave it at that."

"Fair enough." Red looked past Ezra, at the low hills that divided the eastern sky. "Do you have any idea where I can find her?" he asked. "Both of them?"

Ezra looked at Red nervously, as if he was deciding what he should say and how he should say it. Finally, he just shook his head. "I haven't heard even a whisper from her."

Red felt as if a valve had opened somewhere on his body, as if every bit of his battery had just poured out of him. "You're positive?" he asked.

Ezra nodded, and Red reached into his pocket and took out the old Polaroid of Gina.

"Before I go, would you take a look at this?" he asked. "Would you say that's a decent likeness of her? I mean, would the average person be able to recognize her from it?"

Ezra took the photo and held it close to his face. His mouth screwed up on one side, and his eyes narrowed until they nearly closed. "It's taken from pretty far away," he said. "And she's changed some. I can recognize her just fine, but that's because I know it's her." He handed the photo back to Red.

"All right then, Ezra," he said. "And if anything happens to pop into your head, I'm staying at The Top Hat, near the highway exit."

"I know it," Ezra said. "And I will."

"I appreciate it." Red said. "Cause right now, I feel a like a blind man on an Easter egg hunt."

# 8

For a long time, Gretchen never showed much interest in driving. "There's just too much to pay attention to," she'd say. "Kids. Bicycles. Other cars. Not to mention if you got your kid with you. There's just so much that can happen."

While she preferred to let others—Red—do the driving, when Gina came along, she had no choice but to take the wheel, with Red at work and all. Now and then, when the pickup was on blocks in the garage, Grethen would drive Red in the Valiant to his job at the mill, then return at the end of his shift to pick him up. Gina would be there—in the rear seat, waiting for Red as he came out. On days like this, Red liked to swing by the candy machine in the lunchroom and pick up a Hershey's or jellybeans or something for Gina, to have it waiting for her in his lunchpail.

On this particular day, however, Red had been distracted by the sidelining of the green chain that morning. There was a good deal of commotion and paperwork to fill out, and he'd completely forgotten about the candy.

"I'm sorry honey," he said to Gina, tipping his empty pail to show her. "Things got kind of crazy today and I didn't make it to the lunchroom."

"It's okay," she mumbled to him, her face downcast, her lower lip pushed out like a tiny shelf. "You were probably so busy."

"Yeah," he said. He reached back and tousled her hair, and she pulled her lip back into a smile.

"We'll be eating dinner as soon as we get home anyway," Gretchen said, and Red caught wind of it immediately. Sweet, thick. Rum. A knot wound itself in his stomach.

"Hey hon," Red said. "How about I drive us the home?"

"I can do it," Gretchen said. The edges of her mouth curled into a little grin, her eyes lacquered, warm and expectant. "You've had a long day."

Red patted her knee. "It's okay." He opened the door and climbed out, and she slid over to the passenger seat. He decided not to say anything to her in front of the kid. He wanted to believe it was a one-off, that she'd just needed to sand the edges off of a hard day. But, with Gina in the backseat…it couldn't happen again.

They drove up Eighth to Herfy's. The day was still holding onto a little bit of sun, and a few people stood out front, eating burgers or working on their soft serve cones.

Gretchen fished a cigarette from her purse and punched the dashboard lighter with her thumb.

"What do you say we get a cone before heading home," Red announced.

"Come on," Gretchen said. "It'll spoil her dinner."

"No, it won't," Gina chirped from the backseat.

Red glanced into the rearview. Gina was watching him, her eyes wide and eager. He wondered how much she knew at her age. Red wondered how old he'd been when he first understood the meaning of the word sober?

"We'll just be having our dessert first," he said. "Isn't that right, kiddo? You'll eat all your dinner, right?"

Gina nodded her head furiously. The lighter popped from the dash.

"Alright," Gretchen sighed. She took the lighter from the outlet and pressed it to the tip of her cigarette. She gave it a good pull, then let out a billowing cloud of blue. "You win."

Red turned into the parking lot, pulled up to the takeout window and ordered three cones. When they came, he steered over to a spot on the far side of the lot, in the shade of a heavy maple tree. They ate their cones with the windows down, Gina faster than both her parents. Red watched Gretchen, the way she held that cone a little to the side, the way her eyelids weighed heavier than they should have. When she asked how his day had been, he smiled and told her about how he'd been on the green chain, and that there was this new guy, and it hadn't gone well. Gretchen seemed to settle, her eyes clearing up. She laughed when Red described how the fellow had gotten his shirttail tangled in the works, and how it had been a flimsy cotton thing that ripped right off his body and left him half naked.

It was almost seven when they finally got home, the gravel crunching under the tires as Red pulled the Valiant into the driveway, easing it close to the garage door. The sun was sinking low, gold light filtering through the maples. In the back seat, Gina slumped, her hair spilling over her face.

Red cut the engine. In the quiet, he caught it again—the faint tang of alcohol, sharp and sour beneath the smells of oil and dust.

"Go on inside, kiddo," he said, turning toward the back seat.

Gina lifted her head. "Why?"

"Because I said so." His voice had the finality she often

needed. She sighed, pushed the door open, and clomped up the porch steps. The screen door rattled and shut behind her, leaving Red and Gretchen in the cooling dusk.

He turned toward her. "How many?"

Gretchen's eyes narrowed. "How many what?"

"You know what. And don't tell me I'm smelling things, either. I grew up with it."

She gave a short, brittle laugh. "It's all so easy for you, Red. You're gone all day at the mill, making two-by-fours and shooting the breeze with your buddies. Meanwhile I'm the one stuck here trying to wrangle that girl. You think she listens? You think she makes it easy?"

"That your excuse?"

"It's not an excuse." She jabbed a finger against her thigh. "It's survival. It calms me. Helps me not to lose it with her. It's not like I'm blacked out, for god's sake. You don't see me hanging with the winos down at The Townhouse, do you?"

"That's the same damn thing my old man used to say," Red muttered. "Every excuse, long as it wasn't a barstool. Like that made him any less of a drunk."

Her head snapped toward him. "Don't you dare compare me to him."

Red let the words settle, biting back his temper. When he finally spoke, his voice was steady, almost too calm. "I don't want you driving the car if you've been drinking. Not with Gina in it. You hear me? That's not negotiable."

Gretchen scoffed, turning toward the windshield. "Fine," she said, the word thin and sharp. She lit a cigarette, dragging hard.

Red pushed the car door open and stepped out, the gravel crunching under his boots.

Gretchen blew out a stream of smoke that curled around her

face. "I'm going to go inside and take a bath," she said, almost to herself, "if I'm still allowed to do that."

The screen door creaked open. Gina leaned out.

"Inside," Red said, more harshly than he meant to. She disappeared behind the bang of the door.

Gretchen got out of the car and climbed the porch steps slowly, smoldering cigarette in her hand, like a lounge singer making her exit offstage.

Red stood in the driveway for a long while, cicadas buzzing, the porch light now glowing yellow across the yard. Then he climbed back into the Valiant and pulled it into the garage, killing the engine and giving the hood release a tug. He sat in the car for a good moment, staring into the rearview. Seeing that no one was coming, he stepped out into the garage and walked to the front of the car. Lifting the hood, he removed the distributor cap, which he tucked onto a shelf, between the old camp stove and his fishing tackle box.

# 9

The Rockview county sheriff's office was at the south edge of town, where the highway stretched back through the saw-toothed hills toward Spokane. Situated at the end of a juniper-spotted drive and just a short distance from a farmer's co-op, the building was smaller than Red had imagined it would be. It was fashioned like a log cabin, wider than its depth from end to end, with low eaves. From a distance it looked to Red like a striped cake with a green, iced rooftop.

He parked his car close to the front door and climbed out, the sun beating down on him hard as he made his way up the walkway.

It took a little muscle to push through the door, the air conditioner blowing on him like he was in a restaurant cooler when he entered. The space was open, with a grid of a half dozen desks lined from wall to wall, a high counter in the middle blocking visitors from entering the desk area. Only two desks were occupied at the moment, both by men in uniform. One of the men leaned back in his chair with the phone pressed to his ear, while the man at the other desk sat hunched over a yellow legal pad. Along the back wall were a pair of doors framed by frosted glass, the glow of sunlight bleeding through.

A serious-looking woman with jet black hair clipped hard at the shoulders was stationed behind the counter, perched on a low-backed stool. She was reading one of those celebrity gossip magazines, which she snapped closed as soon as Red approached.

"Can I help you?" she said, her lips hardly moving.

"Is there a Deputy Brody available?" Red said.

"Could be," she said evasively. "Is he expecting you?"

"I sure hope so. The name's Red Miller. I talked to him on the phone."

The woman suddenly smiled—not anything forced, Red thought, but definitely not a look that felt natural or comfortable for her. She turned to look over her shoulder and, as if they'd had some secret signal planned, the first officer returned his telephone to its cradle and spun on his chair, nodding to Red. "Mister Miller." His voice reverberated, and Red recalled the phone conversation they'd had. From his living room, Red had imagined he was talking to a fellow his own age or more, with a physical stature to match. However, Brody had to be no more than forty, with a build that was slight and squirrely, probably five and a half feet tops on a good day. His hair was clipped tight around the sides and back, with a little extra on top, parted neatly on one side like a soldier.

"I wasn't expecting you," he said. "Did you say you were coming out?"

Red shook his head. "It was a last-minute kind of thing."

Brody leaned across his desk and began thumbing through a tall stack of papers, finally sliding a weighty folder from the bottom of the stack. "If you like, we can go on back to the conference room," he offered. "It's a bit more private." The woman returned to her magazine, her smile vanishing as she opened up her magazine again.

They went through the glass door on the left, Brody motioning to one of a half dozen chairs crowded around a single rectangular table. A thin row of windows lined the wall near the ceiling, too high to see the outside. "Can I get you anything?" he asked. "Coffee?"

"Water would be great. Something in the air, I think. Maybe pollen."

"More likely hay dust," Brody said. "You're here just in time for the harvest." He leaned out the door. "Verna, some water for Mister Miller, please." He closed the door and took the seat opposite Red, laying the manila folder out in front of him. "I appreciate you coming in, sir," he continued. "I know you've driven a long way."

Red nodded. There wasn't much more to say, really. It wasn't as if there had been any other choice. "I don't suppose you have anything more," he asked. "Since we last talked?"

Brody opened the folder and took out what looked like a driver's license, laminated with a photo in the corner. "Got the verification today from down Washoe County," he said, laying the license on the table.

"Titus Riggs," Red said, reading out the name. The face glared back at him like a mug shot, eyes hard and piercing, with an unkempt mane of jet-black hair that swirled around his head. A single, thick band of eyebrow ran over both of his eyes.

"Reno boy," Brody said. "They know him."

"Titus Riggs," Red repeated. "That's a name all right."

"And he's not familiar to you?"

"Can't say that he is."

"Well, that's a disappointment," the deputy sighed. "I'd hoped otherwise. And anyway, I'm guessing you've had no contact with your daughter since we last talked?"

Red shook his head. "I went by the last address I had for her, but apparently she ain't been there for a good three, four months."

"Was that the complex over on Douglas?"

"I don't remember the street," Red admitted. "A big, shitty blue box next to a cornfield."

"That'd be it," Brody said. "I served the eviction papers back in April. Watched her leave."

The door swung open, and the receptionist swept in, water pitcher in one hand, two glasses pinched between two fingers of the other. She set everything down on the table and poured both glasses half full, seeming to linger in the process, as if she hoped the conversation would just continue.

"Thanks, Verna," the deputy said. He waited until she left, then turned back to Red. "Gina Miller," he said, simple as that.

Red steeled himself for the worst. "So, you knew her," he said.

"Oh yes." Brody smiled, maybe reluctantly, given the way he brought his hand to his mouth. "I got a few stories. If you want to hear them."

Red shrugged his shoulders, then gave a gentle nod.

The officer cleared his throat. "There have been issues here and there in the period of time since she showed up in Rockview," he began. "Drunk and disorderly on a couple occasions. A few shoplifting incidents. Nothing felony level."

Red looked down at the manila folder.

"She sure made use of the charity circuit around town. Churches. The local food bank."

Red looked up sharply at the deputy. "There's nothing wrong with that," he said.

"I wasn't suggesting there is."

"Sounds to me like she was trying to be a good mom to her little boy."

"Of course, Mr. Miller. Look, I didn't mean to come across like I was passing judgement." Brody shifted in his seat. "I was merely trying to—"

"Gina's tougher than any gal you can think of and probably half the men as well…and funny, too," Red began. "She wasn't more than seven when our cat was hit by a car …I brought her with me to this cottonwood grove down a ways from where we lived so we could bury him. Wilfred was its name. The cat. We'd had the thing since she was a baby and Gina was pretty fond of it…We had just laid the body down, all wrapped in a dishrag, in the hole." Red took in a breath. "Gina took hold of my hand, something she didn't do too much. Then she pushed all this air through her teeth and said, 'Well I guess there's no such thing as nine lives, cause I'm pretty sure this is the only time Wilfred ever died.'" Red smiled. "I told her, no, that cats pretty much get one life, just like the rest of us. And she looked up at me with the most serious face you've ever seen and said, 'I'm glad about that, 'cause it would be sad if Wilfred had to get hit by a car eight whole times before he could finally go to heaven.'"

Brody gave a laugh so soft it was almost a whisper. "That is something," he said. He leaned back in his chair and ran his hand over his hair, his thumb seamlessly tracing the part along the left side.

"Do you think it'd be possible for me to have a look at the car?" Red asked, having calmed down.

Brody gave pause for a moment. "I guess I don't see why not," he said finally. "But hang on a second." He got up and went out of the room for a moment, returning with a box the size of a toaster oven. He set it on the table and opened the top. "If you see something you want," he said, "feel free to take it. We've got everything recorded and cataloged by now."

The first thing to jump out at Red was the dog—that damned stuffed dog with the ratty green fur and ridiculous pink ears. It had been ages since he'd laid eyes on the thing, but here it was, as fresh in his mind as the day he watched Gina unwrap the box. He picked it up and turned it over. Considering what its life must have been like in the years since it left Gina's bedroom, it was in pretty good shape, with the exception of an unsettling smear on one side.

"Is this what I think it is?" Red asked, brushing his finger over the fur.

"Blood," Brody said. "We picked it up from the floor of the backseat."

"Jesus!" Red gasped, his hands beginning to tremble.

"Mr. Miller, we've checked all the local hospitals, and no one has a record of a woman matching Gina's description. Or a young, male child." He took the dog from Red and set it down gingerly on the table beside him, as if the thing was asleep and he didn't want to wake it. "Sometimes the smallest cuts bleed like crazy."

"I suppose," Red acknowledged. He wasn't sure whether Brody was being square with him or just trying to keep him from falling apart. He thumbed at the dog's ear again, dry and crusted.

The rest of the box was primarily a mess of junk mail—unopened offers for credit cards, record club and magazine subscriptions. A half dozen or so parking tickets were bunched together at the bottom, along with a letter from a collection agency, a balance due on some rented furniture. There was also a rubber pacifier, caked with dirt, and a single, tiny sock. Along the edge of the box was a laminated card about the size of a credit card. A row of star-shaped holes were punched along the bottom, the word Curl Friends written in red, loopy script over the top.

The address listed a town called Thunder Creek.

"Where's this at?" Red asked.

"It's about midway between here and Spokane," Brody answered. "Right on the highway. But I gave them a call already. She hasn't been in for an appointment in a couple of months. Nothing on the books coming up, either."

Red tucked the card into his shirt pocket. He thought it might be a good idea to pay them a visit anyway. He picked up the stuffed dog and tucked it under his arm. "Did you want me to follow you in my rig? To the car, I mean?"

"You can follow me out the back door," Brody smiled. "Our impound lot is also our motor pool."

They headed down a short, dark hallway to an armored door. Brody gave the push bar a shove, opening up to a gravel lot that extended a good thirty yards to a cluster of hemlock and red cedar. A commercial grade chain-link secured the perimeter, a pair of police cruisers and a panel van crowded near a rolling gate on Red's left. On his right, all alone, sat the Valiant. The front of the car faced the fence line, so the only thing visible was the wide, sharp-edged tail, the chrome lettering spelling out PLYMOUTH. Red could hear Gina's little voice sounding out "Ply-Mouth," as she liked to call the car when she was just learning to read.

Brody led the way down the steps, his arm swinging at his side like he was scattering chicken feed over the ground. As they came upon the car, Red could see the front end clearly now. The windshield seemed to have been peeled from the passenger side and laid on the hood, as if a glass bandage had been partially removed. The front was more "pinched" than crushed, as Red had expected, and he commented as much. "It's a strange set up," he said.

"The thing was wedged between some big old pines," Brody said. "It was almost like she might have made it through if she'd had another two inches on either side."

Red opened the passenger side door and peered inside. A scattering of tiny glass cubes gleamed over the front seats like jewels, contrasted with a single streak of red on the inside of the driver's door. Considering what had happened, it was surprisingly tidy and clean.

The back seat was something completely different, though. Droplets of blood were spotted everywhere, extending over both doors, with a lone stripe over the left side window.

"What the hell is all this?" Red asked. "It's like someone flicked a wet paintbrush back here."

"It's a puzzle all right," Brody said. "And then there's that." He pointed to the edge of the bench seat, at a circle-shaped smudge with four lines extending from it.

"Is that a handprint?" Red asked.

"It appears to be," Brody confirmed. "It's been smeared out, though. So, unfortunately, it's no good for prints."

Red rested his hand on the roof of the car. A sick feeling rose from his gut and began to crawl up into his mouth. "This," he said, waving at the backseat. "If her boy was back there..." He stopped himself, swallowing hard.

"I share the same concern, Mr. Miller," Brody said. "It's why it's imperative that we find her as soon as we can."

They took a few more minutes to walk a wide circle around the wreckage, Red taking in the awful state of things, forcing scenarios in his head that ended with Gina and Noah okay. Outcomes in which they somehow walked away with nothing more than a few minor cuts and secured miracles. It was a tough sell, but it was all he had at the moment.

Finally, he let Brody know he was ready to go. They went back inside, back to the small conference room where Red sat down and took up the water pitcher, refilling his glass and drinking it down in one take. "Do you think you could show me how to find the crash site?" he asked the deputy.

At first Brody didn't answer. He folded his arms over his chest, training his eyes on Red and holding them in place. "We aren't looking for another detective, Mr. Miller," he said finally.

"I'm not looking to be one," Red responded. "I'm just looking for my daughter. And if I never see her again, I'd like to at least see where it all ended for her." His eyes began to well and he looked down sharply, not wanting Brody to see how this was starting to go.

Without saying anything, Brody got up from his chair and left the room, returning with a photocopied roadmap of the state of Idaho. "We're here," he said, drawing a quick circle midway through the state. He scratched an X a couple of inches down. "And this is the hair salon," he said. From there, he traced a line going south, branching off to the southeast. "Look for mile marker 49 and keep an eye out to your right," he said. "Within a hundred yards or so, you'll see it."

"See what?" Red asked.

"There's a stand of pines some distance off the road, and a clear furrow of tracks going straight into them. You can't miss it."

Red stared at the map, considering the distance Gina would have taken from Rockview, and wondering if perhaps he should be looking somewhere else completely. Had she been driving away from her home, or toward it? What the hell had been going through her head?

With nothing more to say, he stood up and shook the officer's hand. "I thank you for your time," he said, adding the request that the deputy give him a phone call if anything turned up, and promising he'd do likewise. Of course, there had been enough times over the years when he'd resolved to do one thing when it came to Gina, only to give up and take the easy way out.

# 10

"This is the last time I'll do this."

Red had issued the warning to Gina in no uncertain terms. The rain poured down in sheets, pinging off the roof of the truck like pellets. He swung open the passenger side door and motioned for her to get in.

Gina got in the car and glanced pitifully at him, her eyes raw, and ringed with clouds of mascara. Sixteen years old and she already had the look of someone twice her age.

"Next time, you can spend the night in jail."

Red kept one hand on the wheel, the other drumming against his thigh. The trestle stretched a good three miles over the slough, the yellow lines blurring under the beams of the truck's headlights. Gina sat with her arms folded tight across her chest, her jaw working at a stick of gum like it was shoe leather.

Neither had said much since leaving the police station. The release agreement sat in the glove box, still warm from the officer's hand.

"You hungry?" Red asked finally, his throat dry and cracking.

"No."

They met the other side of the slough and turned east,

climbing the hill to Highway 9 before Red spoke again. "You know, you keep this up and you're gonna be on a first-name basis with every cop in the state."

Gina let out a jagged laugh. "Wouldn't be the worst thing in the world."

Red tightened his grip on the steering wheel.

Their silence stretched again, broken only by the tires humming over the asphalt. Red thought about letting it drop, the way he always did with her. It would be simpler that way. But this time felt different. Besides the shoplifting bust, and the hour-long drive to collect her from holding, there was something—a kind of weight pressing down on his chest—that pushed him forward.

"Is it about that day?" he asked. "Is that what all this is about?"

"What day?"

He felt a pull at his mouth, like a fish on a hook. Like something trying to draw him away from what he was about to say. He bit down on the inside of his cheek. "That day with your mom," he said, the hook releasing him. "Is that where this is all coming from?"

Gina shifted in her seat.

"The way I handled things that day was wrong," Red continued, his voice low. "I know that."

"Don't," she said, almost in a whisper.

"I shouldn't have acted the way I did. You were just a kid, for god's sake. I should've—"

"Stop!" Gina snapped, cutting him off. "I don't want to talk about it. It was a long fucking time ago, okay? Let's just forget it."

Red looked over at her, but her profile was hard. He swallowed and turned back to the road.

Again, silence, until Red let out a long breath. "I just wish I knew how to do things differently with you. But for some reason you'd rather run the streets than stay with your dad in the house—"

She shook her head. "Look, it's not you, okay? Geez."

"Then what?" His voice cracked before he could catch it.

"I don't know! I just can't stand it there, alright! The house, the town. Everybody looking, everybody knowing your business. Telling you what you should and shouldn't be doing." She let out a quick, bitter laugh. "Even when they're right, I just....It's like something in me wants to do the total opposite. Just to prove I can."

Red nodded slowly, the ache in his chest deepening. He wanted to tell her that he understood, that he sometimes felt the same way when he was her age, when the Army seemed like the only escape. But the words caught in his throat. "Maybe you're not proving anything to anyone but yourself," he said instead.

She didn't answer right away. She pulled her knees up, rested her chin on them, eyes on the dark blur of cedars rushing past the window. "Maybe," she said finally.

The porch light flicked on automatically when they pulled into the driveway, throwing familiar shadows across the front steps. Gina sat in the car for a moment. "Thank you for coming to get me," she said quietly.

Red looked at her, wanting to say always. But all he managed was a tired nod.

And then she was out of the car, walking quickly toward the house, like she couldn't get inside fast enough.

Red stayed in his seat, his hands resting heavy on the steering wheel.

It wasn't more than ten miles until he branched off 95 onto an unmarked road that cut straight through a landscape of open farm fields, clapboard houses and hay bales stacked like toy blocks, nothing close to the pine grove that Brody described. Twice, Red pulled off onto the gravel shoulder to make sure he'd followed the route correctly. After spotting an irrigation ditch that was noted on the map, he continued on, confident that he wasn't more than ten minutes from the site.

He punched the accelerator and let the car float over the plain, and before he knew it, a dark ribbon of trees rose up from the crest of a low slope. He let off the gas as he reached the downhill break, and a parallel set of ruts broke suddenly from the road's edge, black stripes running directly through the rich soil to a thick stand of pines about twenty yards back. A faint pair of tire tracks curved hard from the pavement to the shoulder.

Red steered the truck off the road. Cutting the engine, he rolled down the window, taking in the heady scent of earth and pine for several minutes. The grass stretched beyond the trees, up over the low hills to the west, and the land seemed to breathe with the gentle wind that swept through the cab of his pickup, and out over the plain.

He got out of his truck and ambled slowly toward the pine grove, following the tire tracks. Each step he took offered another possibility that Gina—or whoever the driver might have been—could have done something different. A hard turn in either direction could have circumvented things, depending upon how fast they were traveling. Though a rollover might have been worse.

By now, the sun had dipped below the tops of the pines. At the base of the grove, a dappled shade spread over the ground, a wide skirt of dark and light that danced with the soft movement of the branches overhead. Red could make out the white patches on two of the facing trees, the brutal gouges carved from the Valiant coming to a hard stop between them. It was incredible, Red told himself, that either of the trees was still standing.

The grove continued another hundred feet or so before giving way to the rest of the open field. Just beyond the point of impact was a scattering of smaller trees, and Red imagined that these thin stands would have acted as a breaker of sorts, catching Titus Riggs as he was launched from his seat, through the windshield and out into the night. It would have been grisly, Red thought. Grisly but, hopefully, quick.

He spent a good half hour circling the site, and with the exception of some shards of glass likely from the headlamps, the ground was clean of any debris. If there was blood, it was part of the soil now, blending easily with the carpet of fallen twigs and needles. What looked like footprints were scattered about the grove, though it was impossible to differentiate between what might be the tracks of a person walking away from the crash, and those of the investigators. One thing that Red knew was this: That Gina could have managed to walk away from this, not to mention her little boy, would have been something of a miracle.

He walked over to the twin pines and ran his hand over the exposed wound, picking the shredded bark and splinters from the trunk. "Goddamn it, girl," he said aloud. "What in the holy hell did you do?"

He doubled back toward Rockview, tracing his return route on the map. A few miles before the town, he spotted the salon set back from the highway, positioned between an antique store and a smoke shop. The front picture window was smeared with paint lettering, "Curl Friends," scrawled from pane to pane. Edged up to the front entrance was an old El Camino, no doubt the same one he'd spotted across the street from the motel.

"Well, look at you," Red said, tapping the turn signal and steering into the lot. He took the spot immediately adjacent and got out of his pickup, walking the El Camino's perimeter, taking in the sleek fins, the icy chrome trim and jet-black, glassy finish. He peered through the windshield, at the way the sun captured the metal dog tags that hung loosely from the rearview. "Coincidence?" he asked himself. "I don't think so."

He went inside, nodding to the desk gal as she cradled the phone handset against her neck. She wore a long-sleeved T-shirt with the cuffs of the sleeves cut into fringes, like it had had a near problem with a wood-chipper. Pinned onto her chest was one of those label-maker name tags with KARLA punched out in white block lettering. She had her hair cut short and her fingernails long—not as long as some he'd seen, but up there—and about as pink as pink comes. She held one of them up as if to keep him on pause, then stared down at the receiver as if the person on the other end was sitting right there.

"I know that," Karla said. She looked up at Red and rolled her eyes.

He took a seat in one of the wicker chairs by the big picture window and waited. The place was long and narrow, with a wall of mirrors and four empty chairs along one side and a patchwork of poster-sized photos on the other, pictures of women of various ages and looks, smiling back at him. Some of them sported hairstyles that Red had not seen since before Gina was born.

"Maybe," Karla said into the phone. "Maybe not."

A woman appeared from somewhere in the back, holding a broom. She was a big gal, round in the hips and hind end, and she wore a smock over her shirt, a striped, papery thing that fell over her body like a tent. She'd painted herself up quite a bit, with candy apple red lips and eyelids like two big robin's eggs. Her hair was as blond as Gina's ever was, but she wore hers higher up, kind of ratted and probably sprayed to keep it in place.

"Have you been helped?" she called out. When Red said, "Not yet," she breathed out a sigh and walked over to him, her gait like a penguin's. She narrowed her eyes at Karla, who simply shrugged her shoulders and moved her hand in a rolling motion.

"Were you fixing to get a haircut?" the woman asked, looking over Red's head like she was searching for lice. "We close in half an hour, but I could fit you in."

"No." Red blinked at her name tag. ROSIE. "Is that your El Camino out there?"

She didn't answer at first, instead glancing over his shoulder, in the direction of the picture window. "Why do you want to know?" she finally asked.

He hadn't intended to ruffle feathers, at least not so soon. Besides, his gut told him that letting on that he recognized the car from the motel would throw the whole thing off balance. "I appreciate a good set of wheels, that's all."

She nodded at him slowly, as if peeling through the layers of his explanation. "It's…it's mine."

"1964—Am I right?"

She glanced out the window again, then gave him an up and down look before saying, "You didn't come in here to ask about a car, did you?"

"Actually, I'm looking for someone." He took out the Polaroid of Gina and laid it on the counter. "I was wondering if you might know her." Rosie stared at him at first before finally leaning over to look at the picture, her eyes pinching at the lids. She pulled her lower lip into her mouth and chewed on it just slightly. Finally, she shot a look at Red that seemed to him part knowing, part knife.

"Is that a yes?" he asked.

"What are you, a private eye or something?"

"No."

"Social worker? Child protection?"

"I'm her old man."

"Her old man?"

"Her dad."

"Ah. Well then." She gave a nod of her head and turned and walked to the back of the place, stopping at the last chair and sinking down onto its cushioned seat. She studied Red for a good ten seconds, her gaze moving from his eyes to his mouth to his shoes. "I can tell you she's been in here a couple times," she finally said. "That's about it."

Red considered the card in his wallet, and the row of stamps that had been punched over it. There were more than a couple on there. Still, he didn't feel like pushing that piece just yet.

"She's gotten herself into a bit of trouble," he said. "I'm hoping to get to her before the cops do."

"The cops?"

"Make sure she's okay. Keep the trouble manageable if I can. For her and her boy."

"If you're looking for an address or something, I can't help you there. I told you she's only come in here a couple of times."

"That's what you told me," Red said.

Rosie gave him a hard stare, those blue-painted lids drooping just so. It was as if she was trying to bore straight through his skull with her eyes. "Maybe it was more than a couple of times. She liked to have me do her roots." She brushed her hand over her hair. "When the old color grows out you gotta get your roots done or you start looking like a skunk."

"Did she ever bring her boy in with her?" Red asked.

"She'd sat him down at the toy box over there."

Red looked over to where she was pointing. A single milk crate sat against the wall near the entrance, brightly colored plastic toys peeking through the sides.

"When would you say she was in last?"

Rosie shrugged, exhaled an irritated sigh, then went to the station behind her and pulled out a notebook. She flipped it open and thumbed through the pages. "March 12th."

"You're sure?"

"Yeah, I'm sure." She turned the notebook to him and pressed her thumb to one of the squares. Written in ballpoint next to 2:00 was Gina Miller. "I do remember she came in the same car that's in that picture you showed me, and Noah was with her." She seemed to catch herself then, glancing up at Red for a quick instant. "Her boy," she added.

"Yeah, I know his name," Red said. "I'm surprised you remembered it, seeing's how she only came in a couple of times."

"Well," she stammered. "Like I said, it might have been more than that. I remembered his name cause of the ark." She gestured toward the toy box, and Red could see the edge of what looked like a ship poking from the top. "He liked to play with the animals. I thought it was funny, with the name and all."

Red considered all of this, and though he thought there might be details in that head of hers that were still unsaid, he couldn't see a way to push harder without blowing it all up. He thanked her for her time and gave her the name to the motel if she thought of anything else and was willing to tell him. "I'm just really worried about her," he said. "The two of them."

"Yeah," she said. "I can imagine."

As he turned to leave, she called out to him. "It's tough being a single mom. She's doing the best she can..."

Red didn't say anything to that.

"Well, anyway," she added. Then she turned and disappeared into the back.

As Red walked past Karla on his way out, she gave off a loud, long cackle. "You're a lying sack of shit," she laughed into the phone. "I friggin' love it."

# 11

It was later than usual when Red came home. A last-minute sick call had created an opening in the swing shift at the mill, and he was happy to get the overtime. He hadn't expected Gretchen to still be awake.

Except for the under glow of the kitchen hood light, and the steady orange pulse of the cigarette Gretchen seemed determined to finish, the house was dark. She stood at the sink in her bathrobe, hair twisted up in some colored clips, staring down into the drain like it held some kind of answer for her. Her robe was open at the chest, more tawdry than anything.

Red set his keys down quietly, not wanting to startle her. Still, she turned quickly when she heard him. "You're home," she said. There was a cup on the countertop beside her—one of those little aluminum tumblers. Behind it, a bottle of something he hadn't purchased. There was a second tumbler too, upside down on a dishtowel like it had been considered, then abandoned. Maybe she'd meant it for him. Maybe she just didn't want it to look like she was drinking alone. She noticed Red staring at it. "It was one of those days," she said. "Gina." Gretchen moved to one side, the bottle disappearing behind her. "One thing, then another." Her shoulders slumped in a way that wasn't so much tired, but loose. As if her bones had all given up for the night but hadn't told her yet.

Her cigarette burned brighter for a second, then dropped from her fingers into the sink, where it hissed against the water. She swayed ever so slightly. The small movement might have just been simple breathing, but Red understood what it could mean, and just how quiet something could get before it started to fall apart.

He came back into Rockview as the sun touched the western range. As he took one turn after another through and around town, he found himself searching every parking lot and alcove, hoping that she might make a sudden appearance. But before long one place blurred into the next, and Red drifted into what felt like a waking dream. Faces turned to watch him as he drove past, couples elbowing one another and pointing at him, as if they were all playing a part in the adventure he'd placed himself in. Of course it was not like that at all. Or maybe it was. It was getting late, and in spite of the few pieces of information he'd managed to gather, he was no closer to knowing where she and Noah were.

He pulled into the lot of a True Value, parking next to a little taco stand that was set up along the fence line. He went up to the counter and pointed to a burrito wrapped in tin foil in a glass case, then swapped a few dollar bills for some quarters and nodded his thanks before walking across the lot to a payphone tacked to the front of the hardware store. He dialed Linda's number and waited while the operator told him how much change to drop in. The phone on the other end rang once, then a second and third time. He took a glance at his watch and noted it was just eight-thirty. What would she have going on that would take her out of the house at that hour? Just as he was about to hang up, the machine picked up.

Hello friends, her voice said. It was all velvet and sugar—even as a recording, her voice had a way of calming his racing heart. Sorry I missed your call because doggone it, I really want to talk to you! Well, you know what to do.

"Honey it's me," he said after the beep. "I don't have a whole hell of a lot to share other than that I've been chasing my tail like a dog ever since I got here. She ain't making it easy on me, but then she never did. If you get a minute give me a call at the motel later tonight." He leaned against the wall of the hardware store, pressing his head to the bricks behind him. "I'm thinking I'll spend tomorrow driving around, and if nothing turns up, probably head on home. I don't know what else to do."

He hung up the phone and walked back to his pickup. By now there were a bunch of folks crowded around a pair of picnic tables in front of the taco stand. Red unwrapped his burrito and took a healthy bite, thinking it was the best damned thing he'd eaten all week.

There was a big station wagon parked opposite him, a clutch of kids inside, the doors wide open like wings. One of the kids, a little girl of perhaps seven or eight, jumped out and took off running toward the taco stand. She was shouting something Red couldn't make out—Spanish, probably. A man, probably just a little younger than Red, stood leaning against the stand talking to the guy behind the counter. The man turned to look at the girl as she came to him. She said something again, and he swept her up in his arms, propping his elbow under her like she weighed nothing.

After Gretchen died, there was a stretch of time when Red

tried to be better about giving Gina the kind of affection he knew was important for a child to have. He'd rest a hand on her shoulder when it was time for bed, or hold her in a sort of "half hug" when she came home from school, if she allowed him to. It wasn't something that came natural to him, and up to then Gretchen had been the one to fill that need for the most part. Red hadn't been raised to hold or cuddle. His own mother gave affection like he was a bed to be made, tucks and pats and smooths, her hands on him only out of necessity, to straighten him, or send him on his way. As far as his father was concerned, touch was predominately disciplinary and corrective, or an occasional clasp on his shoulder if the moment called for validation.

So touching Gina was something Red often had to force himself to do, not because doing so was unpleasant but, rather, because it just didn't feel a part of who and what he was. You might as well have told him to put his underclothes on the outside of his trousers.

But it was important, he knew. For her. And so he tried like hell to do it.

The truck rolled easily into the parking lot of The Top Hat, and Red took the open stall closest to the courtyard entrance. Things were pretty quiet—a few of the rooms had their windows lit up behind pulled drapes, and there wasn't the slightest whisper of either mariachi music or shouting kids.

The glow of the pool lights rippled over the cement walls. Near the pool steps, Sadie lay stretched on a reclining patio seat, under a fringed umbrella with a tall glass of something at her elbow.

"Looks like it's happy hour," Red said.

"I'd say it's past time," she said. "I notice you're solo."

"So are you."

"Morris is down for the night, assuming he stays in bed. I got a bell on the door in case he gets to roaming. Anyway, how was your day?"

Red laughed softly, shook his head. "Long story."

"Long night ahead if you feel like talking." She lifted her glass and took a drink. "I might not have answers, but I got ears."

"Whatcha drinking?"

"Seven and Seven," she said. "I've got plenty if you'd like to partake."

"Partake I will." Red pulled a chair from the deck and sat opposite her, on the other side of the little table. His stomach gave a tumble then, maybe stress, maybe the burrito.

Sadie said, "I tell you, when this week is over, if I don't eat another tortilla for the rest of my life I'll be just fine." She reached under her chair and produced a box of cake donuts, flipped the lid and offered one up.

"Don't mind if I do," Red said.

She leaned over and reached into the cooler, and then came the sound of ice against glass, and the pop of a soda can. "How are you holding up? she asked.

"Better than I ought to be," he replied.

She handed him a tumbler, already wrapped in condensation. "To happy hour," she said.

"To no more tortillas," he grinned, then took a quick sip, and the whole thing seemed to wash over him like a baptism. He could feel her watching him. "Honestly," he said, "the day's been something of a cluster fuck—pardon my French."

She took another drink from her glass, then leaned back in her chair and gave a thumbs up. "That's the only kind of French I know," she reassured.

"I'm trying to track down my miscreant daughter. It seems there was a car crash, some guy pitched from the passenger seat through the windshield. It was her car but there's neither hide nor hair of her to be found."

"Jesus, that's tough," Sadie said. "If they didn't find her, they figure she's alive, right? That's good news?"

Red shrugged his shoulders. "I hope to hell so. To make matters worse, there's a kid in the mix."

Sadie closed her eyes tight and shook her head slowly.

Red continued. "Grandson, two years old. Damned if I knew a thing about him till just now." He took a good swig of his drink. "You're probably wondering what kind of man doesn't even know he's got a grandson, but I ain't had more than a handful of conversations with Gina in the last few years."

"I got nothing to say other than shit happens." Sadie set her empty glass down on the ground and set to mixing another drink. "Families are anything but simple."

"The lack of communication wasn't my doing," Red said. "She's a tough nut, always was. And a runner. Hell, even before my wife died and she started taking to the hills every time she heard the word 'no,' she'd shut herself in her room if she didn't get her way. Push the chair in front of the door to try to keep us out, and there she'd stay till she fell asleep. A few times I considered busting down the door. Never did, though. Could've made things even worse. So I just stood outside it until I quit hearing movement and figured she was sleeping."

"Don't be too hard on yourself. For a young girl heading straight into puberty, nothing in life is fair and the whole world is stacked against you."

Red smiled at this. "I suppose so."

"I grew up in a house with a lot of noise. It wasn't all bad noise, but there were times when it sure as hell felt like it. I used to line my bedroom closet with blankets and close myself in there with a flashlight and a book. Sometimes, I'd fall asleep there, wake up hours later."

"How did your folks handle that?"

Sadie shook her head. "I'm not sure they ever even knew about it. I'd come out when I felt like it and everyone would just be carrying on the same."

Red considered this for a moment, but couldn't shake the feeling that Gina's behavior was more than just the landmines of adolescence. The stubbornness, penchant for escape. Gretchen's drinking. There could have been different choices on his part that might have made things easier for her, for all of them. "I like to think I did my best," he said. "I provided a decent home. Told 'em I loved 'em more times than anyone ever said it to me. I sure as hell never hit anyone." He raised his glass to his lips and downed the final drops.

"Let me take care of that for you." Sadie took the tumbler from him and started working on a refill. "If you spend the whole time staring at the rearview mirror, it's gonna be a short trip off a high cliff," she said. "Look at it for quick checks. Don't forget what's behind you, but keep your eyes on the road because what matters more than anything is what's coming up."

She handed him a fresh drink. "It ain't easy to take my eyes from that mirror," he said. "Lots of should-haves there to distract." He took a big sip.

"Well, you're here," she said. "That says something."

There was a sudden coughing sound, and Red noticed that the door to Sadie and Morris' room was ajar. Sadie looked over her shoulder, held her gaze there for a moment, then went back to her drink.

"How long has he been like that?" Red asked.

"You mean how long has he been like this?" she asked, circling her fingers over her temple. "In one way or another, a good ten years. Maybe longer. But I'd say things really took a turn in the last year or so."

"I'm sorry to hear it," he said. "I've seen it here and there with old folks and it ain't any fun."

"The funny thing is," she said, "in my case it's a strange complication. I mean, don't get me wrong—it's hard watching him go this way. Forgetting all the things you or I take for granted. How to fasten a belt. Tie your shoes. The sequence of things that need to happen just to sit down and take a shit." She laughed. "Get one of those steps out of order and it ain't pretty."

Red laughed with her. "I never thought of that."

"Neither did I." She looked back at the room again. "But otherwise, I'm finding myself in this weird place of enjoying a father who is a hell of a lot different from the father I grew up with. The old fucker in there is nothing but smiles and sunshine, always with a sweet story to tell, quick to give a 'thank you' and a compliment, even when there's nothing requiring it." She swirled her finger through her drink. "The other day he asked me what my name was again and when I told him, he said 'I think I got a daughter named Sadie.' I didn't say anything to correct him, and then he said 'I sure miss her. She was the best kid you could ever have.'" Her voice seemed to catch. "I call it my 'curious gift,'" she said with a smile. "It's like all the old roads in his brain have been scrambled and rerouted the way they were supposed to have been. It's not expected that we ever get a second chance at something like this. A chance to kind of do everything all over again, if that makes sense."

Red nodded at this. It did make sense. If only someone could figure out how to do something like that before it was too late.

At that, there was a ringing sound behind him and he quickly realized it was the phone in his room. He thanked Sadie for the drink and the talk, then hustled to his room and picked up the receiver. "Hello," he said.

"Oh, I'm glad I caught you." It was Linda, and she talked as if she was out of breath. "I got your message. I was out shopping and lost track of time."

Just the sound of her voice felt like a blanket draped snugly over his shoulders. "I appreciate you calling me back, hon," he said. "It's been a hell of a day."

"Do you want to tell me about it?" she said.

"I don't want to cripple your phone bill," he sighed. "Let's just say I probably looked at every square inch of this town and there ain't so much as a strand of hair that belongs to her." He lay down on the bed, fished for the television remote and clicked on the tube. There was a sitcom playing, a show he'd caught a few times about a young gal from a small town who moves to the big city and can't seem to figure it all out. The girl was on a date with some clean-cut fellow and while Red couldn't hear what was being said, the audience laughter punched in and out.

He gave Linda an outline of where he'd been—the apartment, police. The crash site. The hair salon. "I'm gonna give it a couple more days, I think," he said. "Follow up on a few things."

"Do you want me to come out there?" she asked.

"No, no," he said, though the thought of having her there settled him some.

"Are you sure? I could leave in the morning and be there by lunchtime."

"There's nothing for you to do here."

"Sometimes just being with somebody is doing enough," she reminded him.

He sat with that for a moment, and while he couldn't find reason to disagree, he didn't want to burden her, and he told her as much.

"The second anything with you feels like a 'burden' I'll let you know," she said.

Just then there was knock at the door. Red instinctively looked over to the opposite wall as if he could see through to the outside.

"Somebody's here," he said. "Probably the gal next door."

"The gal?" Linda said. "I guess I'm definitely coming out, then."

"Settle down," he said to her. "She's here with her old man, on a short vacation from the nursing home."

The knock came again. "Mr. Miller?" It was a man's voice. "It's me, Ezra. Can we talk a minute?"

Ezra.

"Jesus," Red said, "It's that kid from the feed store."

"Who?"

"The one who ran around with Gina."

"Oh, Red," Linda said. "Call me right back."

Red hollered that he'd be right there, then hung up the phone and went to the door.

# 12

Red opened the door and there was Ezra, hay bale hair parted crisp along one side, the whole thing combed down tidy as a kid on his first day of school. He'd traded his hayseed for a sharp denim jacket and blue jeans with a belt buckle the size of a police badge.

"Sorry to just show up like this," he said. In one hand he held a set of keys that he twirled around his index finger like a toy. "I figured it was better if I just came by. I got your room number from Chip at the front desk."

"Chip?"

"We went to school together."

"Okay," Red said. "So, I'm assuming you wanna talk?" Red walked away from the door and Ezra came inside. There were two chairs in the room, around a small table. Ezra sat on one side of the table, while Red pulled the other chair a good distance back. He sat down and stretched his legs out. Something told him this would take some time.

"I'm guessing you still ain't found her," Ezra asked.

"You're guessing right."

Ezra worked the breast pocket of his jacket and took out a pack of Winstons. "You mind?"

"Be my guest."

Ezra drew out a smoke and pulled a little glass ashtray on the table to him. "I've cruised by this place probably a hundred times but have never been inside," he said, taking a scan of the room. "It's nicer than I pictured it. From the street it looks like a dump, if you want my honest opinion."

"It's all right," Red said.

"Still, you oughta check for bedbugs if you haven't already," Ezra added. "I could show you how if you don't know..."

"I don't imagine you came here to advise me on motel cleanliness."

Ezra's mouth broke into grin. "No sir, I did not. Truth is, I wasn't being completely straight with you before." He looked down at his black cowboy boots, as if he was preparing for a scolding.

"I wondered," Red said.

"Yeah, well after you left, I got to feeling bad about it. Here you drove all the way from the other side of the mountains. As long as I've known Gina, I never knew anyone who cared enough about her to do something like that." He snapped the lid of his Zippo and lit up the cigarette, giving away a slight tremor in his hand as he did so. He took in a hearty drag, held it in for a moment, then pushed it out the side of his mouth. "I actually ran into her a couple of months ago, at the minimart before you take the exit from the highway into town. I pulled up into the parking stall right next to her before I even realized it was her. She was riding shotgun in that Rambler of hers. We talked for a few minutes."

"You mean Valiant." Red corrected.

Ezra stopped, screwed up his face. "Valiant?" he asked. "I thought it was a Rambler."

Red shook his head. "They're similar."

"Damn," Ezra said. "That's something. Anyway, I guess she'd been seeing this guy, a dude named Titus. I don't know him, but I heard a few things from people who did."

"What about him?"

"He'd hitchhiked up from Reno not too long before he met Gina. The general consensus on Titus is that he's a grade A asshole. I told Gina I'd heard some things about him, and she told me that whatever I heard was probably true and that it didn't matter anyway because she was getting ready to move on from him." Ezra added that Gina, Titus and Noah had been living on this rhubarb farm out in a place called Midvale. "They'd made plans once to move down to Boise after the rhubarb season wound up, but pretty soon it was obvious that it wasn't the dream come true she thought it would be. Plus, the way he was treating Noah was pretty rough."

Red leaned in. "What kind of rough?"

"She didn't say much about it. Just that he'd swat his butt if he got fussy. Call him names. That kind of stuff."

"Sounds like this Titus fella could've used a good, swift kick in the ass," Red said. It also sounded like Ezra didn't know about Titus' unfortunate demise.

Ezra laughed in agreement, took a drag from his smoke and tipped his head back, blowing a gray cloud into the pendant lamp that hung from the ceiling above them. "She had a call into this gal named Junebug who runs a sober house just outside the city proper. Rents rooms to women stuck in a hard spot. Gina told me she was gonna give her a call, see if she had space for her and Noah."

Sober house. Red liked the sound of that.

"Right about then Titus came out of the store and she didn't want to talk any more. I told her good luck with everything, and then I tore the hell out of there before he could lay his eyes on me."

Red let this roll around in his head some, Gina making plans to move on yet again, but then changing it all up. Choosing sane over crazy, for once. Red felt as if a balloon was being inflated inside his chest.

"I have my own confession to make," he said suddenly. "I'm afraid I wasn't completely straight with you before, either."

"That so?" Ezra said, eyebrows reaching upward.

"There was an accident about a week ago. Gina ran her car into some trees about halfway between here and Spokane. Left the scene. It's why I got a call from the police. It's why I'm here at all, to try and find her and Noah, make sure they're okay."

Ezra sat back in his chair and ran his hand over his face. He gazed past Red, as if he was viewing the whole scene as it unfolded in front of him. Red watched closely, unsure if this response was genuine or just a piece of theater. "Isn't that something," he finally said.

"I'm surprised you didn't know," Red replied, and before he could even mention Titus' journey through the windshield, Ezra shook his head like he was shaking the entire story from his mind.

"Anyway, I gave Junebug a call before I came here," Ezra said. His eyes held steady on Red's, as if he was counting every blink, every twitch. "She hasn't seen either Gina or Noah since maybe a week, week and a half ago."

"Goddamn it," Red seethed, pulling in what felt like half the air in the room. It seemed like every time he found himself close to something promising, another roadblock went up. He let out his breath in a long, slow exhale.

Ezra tapped the ash loose from his smoke into the tray.

"Gina's stuff is still there, though," he said. "The place is not so far from here, just past the old flour mill on Monroe Street." He said it like MUN-roe. "I asked Junebug if I could bring you by, and she said it was fine by her."

Red straightened up in his chair. "When?"

"Whenever you want, but my advice is right now. Junebug's good people but she can be flaky. Her mind changes like the temperature."

Red looked over at the telephone on the nightstand. The thought of Linda expecting to hear from him and him not calling tugged at his stomach. But it was already after nine, and if he was going to see this Junebug gal, time was a factor. Linda would understand when all was said and done. What did he have to tell her at the moment anyway?

Next door, the sound of brass instruments suddenly rose up, thrumming through the wall. Ezra straightened up in his chair. "Sounds like that's our cue to go."

It was all of a ten-minute drive from The Top Hat to the far edge of town. They took Ezra's truck, and he narrated the whole journey, like some overzealous tour guide. There were strip malls that had once been playfields, playfields that had once been trash-filled, vacant lots. The local school was a flat, brick structure that took up a whole city block. Ezra told Red that he had attended from kindergarten through eighth grade. "The high school is about a mile on the other side of town, which is a good thing. You'd be surprised how many of those guys would manage to find themselves over here at lunchtime, standing at the fence and calling out to the middle school girls."

The very thought gave Red's stomach a kick. That would be Gina without a doubt, bouncing on her toes and running straight for that fence.

They drove past the school and then took a combination of lefts and rights that Red quickly lost track of. Finally, at the end of an asphalt street, lined on either side with a run of stucco-coated bungalows, they came to a stop at a four-way intersection. "My cousin was killed right here," Ezra said suddenly. He stared past Red, at the roadway kitty corner from where they were. A thin poplar tree stood there like some traffic cop, branches hanging limply out from its trunk. "He got hit by a van that blew right past the stop sign." Ezra's mouth curled. A smile more from courtesy than anything else. "I was right over there," he said, pointing in the direction of the tree. "Saw it all happen and I swear to God Jerry was like a rubber toy bouncing right off the front end of the car."

Red could see tears starting to pool in Ezra's eyes. "Damn, kid," he said, trying to be reassuring. "That's hard."

Ezra quickly wiped his eyes with the palm of his hand and stepped on the gas, the doomed intersection fading from sight in Red's sideview mirror.

Soon, the towering columns of a high structure glowed white in the truck's headlights. The flour mill, Red assumed. Ezra reached into his jacket pocket and retrieved the pack of Winstons, tamping the square against his knee. "Almost there," he said, nodding his chin toward the road ahead. "Just past the mill."

They bounced over a railroad crossing and then just past the mill the roadway split into a Y. Ezra steered the pickup onto the smaller of the two streets, and the road surface reduced itself to gravel, the shocks beneath the car overworked by the ruts and rocks. Off to the right, a row of dimly lit windows stared back at Red through a few low, leafy trees.

The single-story house sat on a large lot. The place looked lopsided, like one end was sinking into the ground. A large, overgrown shrub appeared to be consuming the right corner, as if a giant bite had been taken out of it. Behind drawn drapes, the blue static of a television flickered blue to white, then blue again. The surrounding landscape was not much more than patches of crabgrass, growing here and there in tufts like small, green explosions.

"So, this is where she's been staying?" Red asked.

"Up till a week or so ago," Ezra said. "Junebug can fill in the gaps."

They came up to the dirt walkway together. Ezra stepped past Red to the front door and rapped on the sidelight window, then pushed open the door with a nudge of his knee.

A woman stood in the kitchen in the back, her hands gripping the frame of a metal walker. She had on a bathrobe that was cinched around her ample waist, a velour thing that seemed to catch the overhead light in an odd way, like a sort of sheen washing down over her body.

"You sure got here quick," she said, turning to them. Her words fell into one another and for a moment Red thought she might have been lost halfway in the bottle. It was when she said, "So you must be Gina's dad," that Red realized she was talking without the benefit of teeth, real or false.

"I am," Red answered. Ezra went inside, Red following close behind.

Despite it being the middle of summer, the baseboard heater along the far wall of the living room clicked away. The thick heat, along with the underlying odor of something recently fried, wrapped itself around Red like a dog blanket.

Junebug shuffled her way into the living room. "From what

Ezra tells me, I'd venture to bet you've had a rough couple of days."

"Truer than you can imagine."

"I can imagine quite a bit."

The noise from the television began to play games with Red's attention, the racket of tires squealing and shots being fired, people shouting over one another. As if she'd read his mind, Junebug pushed her way past and reached over to turn the volume down. Onscreen, cars continued to slide around street corners, bystanders diving into bushes and alleyways like gymnasts, only now in silence.

Junebug walked over to the lumpy couch and sat down with a pronounced sigh. She motioned toward Red. "Sit down," she said. "I got no roaches or spiders, I promise."

Red took a seat on the armrest. Ezra hung back by the front entrance, leaning against a wall.

"You think I'm kidding," Junebug added. "It might not be tidy in here but it's not dirty." She reached over to the side table at her elbow and picked up a large tumbler of something, taking a good-sized drink and setting it back down, pulling her lips back so that Red caught a glimpse of the light against her gums.

"So, I'm told that Gina's been staying with you?"

Junebug took a breath and started to answer, but then something seemed to catch in her throat, setting off a round of deep, horsey coughs. After another healthy swig of her drink, she tapped her fist to her chest. "Up till last week, yeah. Her and the little one." She moved her jaw from side to side, her lips reaching back over those gums of hers. "Noah."

Just hearing that much made Red feel a gentle wash, a sensation that he was closer to Gina than he had been in some time. Up until last week would put her here right up to the accident. At least for a little while this had been her home, and this woman had shared it with her and Noah.

"I got a few extra bedrooms I rent out from time to time," Junebug said. "I used to allow weekly, but the kind of stuff that came with it wasn't nothing but aggravation. All that traffic in and out, women running away from men, then running straight back to them the next day. Gina showed up at my door a couple months ago carrying everything she had in a garbage bag with that boy at her side. Normally I don't like to have kids in the house."

"But you made an exception."

"Yeah."

"Why?"

"I don't know. He was a cute little thing," she said, showing her gums in a smile. "And I could tell he was good boy. He kept himself busy the whole time we was talking, and then when I got up to put on something to eat, he was right there at my knee, wanting to help me out. I couldn't understand half of what came out of his mouth but hell, people only ever understand half of what I say." She folded her arms over her chest. "And anyway, I could tell the boy might do good with some quiet in his life. That fellow she had with her, what was his name?" She looked over at Ezra.

"Titus," he said.

"Titus," Junebug repeated. She shook dramatically as if she'd just come in from the cold. "He made a couple comments, like would I let him stay here with them. Trying to butter me up, calling me ma'am and all that. I told him nothing personal, but I don't allow men to stay in my home, no matter who. My house, my rules. I was afraid there might be a conflict when I told him that, but I didn't care, because I didn't like him, didn't like the way he talked to them."

"How did he talk to them?" Red's jaw tightened, his teeth pressing against one another.

"It's difficult to explain. Not so much the words he said but how he said them. Everything was bossy. Hard."

"He never hit her though," Red asked.

"I asked her that and she said 'no,'" Junebug said. "When I told her I had an ex-husband who knocked me around, she said if any guy ever hit her, he'd get that one shot and one shot only."

"She said that?" Red asked.

Junebug nodded. "I only asked because there was times he seemed to be getting riled up. Swagger and all, and I've seen that kind of thing before. But she insisted she wasn't having any of it."

Red took this in, the familiar red line that Gina always held to, even though there never seemed to be other red lines in her life.

Junebug took in a deep breath and let it out slowly. "So, the last night she was here he'd come around sometime close to dark," she resumed. "We were all getting ready for bed. He made a circle around the whole house, knocking on the windows and yelling for Gina to come out, saying he wasn't gonna leave till she did. I told her not to say anything and then I went to my closet and got out my gun. Now it's just a twenty-two and everyone knows you can't do as much to a grown man with a twenty-two that you could with a thirty-six or a forty-five. Unless you're a really good shot, and even though it's been a while, I can tell you I'm a pretty darned good shot." She glared at Red, as if he might need more convincing. "Gina hollered at him to settle down, that there was no need to act like an animal, that she'd meet him on the porch. She told me she was sorry, that she didn't want all this on my shoulders. 'I'll take care of it,' she said. Then she went out to talk with him for a few minutes, came in and told me they were going someplace, asked if I could watch Noah for a bit."

"And you did?"

"Sure." She looked over to Ezra for some reason, and he gave her a smile.

"Anyway, it got pretty late. I put Noah down and then turned in myself. Later on, I don't know, maybe a few hours, I heard Gina come in. She came to my bedroom and said that she was back but was going out again, but this time she was gonna take Noah with her and for me not to worry. Said she'd call me." Junebug shook her head. "It was dark, but I could see outside my window to the street. There was a car idling at the curb. I figured it was her car but seeing's how apparently her car was up against some trees by then, who knows whose car it was."

"So, it sounds like you heard the news, then," Red said. "About the accident."

Junebug sat up straight, shot a furtive glance to Ezra. "I got wind of something."

Red clenched his hands together, pressing his fingers into his knuckles until they hurt. "And that was it?" he said. "That was the last you saw of them?"

"Yes."

Red stood up. "Well, that sure is something," he said. "I do appreciate it, though. You taking care of her and all." He looked down a long hallway to the back of the house. "Ezra said her room still has all her things in it?"

"Her room?"

"Just a quick peek, please."

Junebug shifted her body nervously. "She's got the padlock still on it. And since it's only been a week since I last saw her… and she's paid up through the month…" She looked over at Ezra, her face drawn now, as if she'd just disappointed everyone in the room. "I'm not sure if it'd be right."

"Well, I don't know…the law," Ezra said, drawing out his words. "If she abandoned it and hasn't even called you…The property owner ought to be able to get in. Make sure everything's okay."

"I won't touch anything," Red promised. "If she comes back, it'll all still be there exactly like she left it."

"I don't want to make trouble…"

"Ma'am," Red began. "If you knew…" He paused, his throat tightening.

"She's in some trouble, Junebug," Ezra interrupted. "You know how these local cops can be. Now, Mister Miller, he's come all the way from west of the mountains to try and find her and the boy. To try and fix whatever mess she's got herself in. And anyway, he's probably the only one looking that even gives a good goddamn about her."

Junebug sucked in her breath and held it there, looking from Red to Ezra, then back again. Finally, she gave exhaled, long and full.

"You're not gonna rip the hell out of my door, are you?"

Ezra retrieved a crowbar from his truck, and it took him less than thirty seconds to pry the padlock from the frame. He left behind a few holes that he promised to patch with putty or toothpaste or whatever he could scare up.

"It's fine," Junebug said. She went back to the living room, dialing the volume back up on the television and sinking down onto the sofa.

Red entered the bedroom. It was so unlike what Gina's teenage bedroom had looked like when she was growing up.

Where there had once been posters of rock bands and teen idols, the walls here were mostly bare, with the exception of a small space over the headboard of the twin bed, where a few pictures cut out from magazines had been taped up. Mountain scenes, some flowers. There was a nice photo of an elk herd in the snow. The bed was made up neatly, with a little stuffed rabbit on one of the pillows. Red picked up the animal and held it to his nose, taking in the musty scent. He figured it had belonged to Noah, who had left it behind in whatever frenzy or mishap had taken him and his mother from this place.

As Red stood there, the old Gina eventually began to materialize. On the far side of the bed, which he hadn't seen from the door, a pile of clothing. Jeans, a discarded bra, a plaid flannel shirt. And the smell of perfume and cigarettes, just as it had been in those teenage years, when she thought she could mask the odor of smoke with a few sprays of cheap, Pay n' Save cologne.

The closet slider was open most of the way, and there was a little bedroll that Red assumed had been Noah's. A blanket, too, sporting cartoon characters that Red recognized from Saturday morning programs he'd wake up to, Gina still in her nightgown, cross-legged in front of the screen with a heaping bowl of cereal on her lap. Red caught himself in a smile.

There was a single dresser against the wall, tall and slender, coated in thick white paint that was chipped at the edges. A wind-up clock sat on top, next to a wooden box. Red had seen the box before, in his house, then again in a little apartment that Gina had lived in for a short time in Ash Falls, before she hit the road with Frankie. It seemed strange that she would have left it here.

He tipped the lid open and rifled through the contents. There was some jewelry, nothing valuable-looking, though he would be the first to admit that he didn't have an eye for that kind of stuff. One of the rings he recognized as having once belonged to Gretchen. It had been a gift that Red had given to Gina on her sixteenth birthday, a gesture that he'd hoped might do something to help matters at the time. A sort of "restart." It brought a smile from her and a thanks, but that was it. Still, he was glad to see that she had held unto it .

The box also contained a few photos of Gina at various places in the years since he'd last seen her. She looked more or less the same, that hair of hers still bottle-blond. In one photo, however, Gina was with a little fellow that could only be Noah, and it dawned on Red that this was the first time he'd seen what the boy looked like. He took in a breath. Holy moly, he thought, what a handsome little guy. Eyes dark and serious, and a head of hair that Red could only dream of having, thick and ringed with curls. Gina held him on her lap and was pointing at something or someone, the camera maybe. Both mother and son had banner smiles, and it buoyed Red to know that in that moment, when the camera's button had been pressed, they were happy.

As Red went to close the lid, a flash of color caught his eye. At first glance he thought it was a poker chip, which would have made sense given Gina's familiarity with casinos. He picked it up and turned it over in his hand. Then he recognized it. The color red, a celebration of one month of sobriety, the big triangle with the mantra, TO THINE OWN SELF BE TRUE, printed along the edge. "Well, I'll be damned," he said aloud, and while he understood there was a lot here to be considered, there was also plenty to wonder about. That a commitment had been made and kept, even if only for a short time. While there was no way of knowing if this had been months (or even years) before, a month is a month.

Red slipped the photo of Gina and Noah into his shirt

pocket and closed the lid to the box. When he turned to leave the room, there was Ezra in the doorway, hands deep in his pockets, eyebrows arched, a half grin on his face.

"You find any of what you were looking for?" he asked.

"There was never a list in my head," Red said. "But I'm a few steps higher up now than when I came, so that's a win."

Before leaving, Red thanked Junebug for her hospitality. "I don't know how she'll take my being here if she comes back," he warned.

"I never did plan on telling her," Junebug said. "So as long as nobody here says anything, she don't need to know. Believe me, I need conflict like I need one less tooth in my head."

Red paused at the front door. "There's an important detail about the crash that I'm guessing neither of you know about," he said. Then he went through the story again, only this time he added the part about Titus going through the windshield.

"You're shitting me," Ezra said. "Goddamn."

"Well, I'll be darned," Junebug added. "But nothing about Gina and the boy?"

"Nope. It's why I'm here," he said. "But so far I can't find a single person who's seen or heard from her since."

"Well, I do hope you find your girl, Mister Miller," Junebug said. "For her sake and for the boy's."

They pulled out onto the road, and before long the whine of a train whistle cut the air. In the distance, Red could see an endless line of railcars clicking through the trees.

"Damn it," Ezra said. "We'll be sitting there forever from the looks of it." He came to the Y in the road and hooked a hard left, taking the route opposite from before. "There's a detour we can take if we hurry," he said. "Get ahead of it and cross at the Danforth junction."

"It's okay to wait," Red found himself saying. "I ain't in any rush."

"It's cool," Ezra said, giving Red a reassuring smile. "I do this all the time."

He punched the accelerator, kicking up a fishtail of gravel. As the road straightened out it began to run parallel to the train, and they drove on like that, passing railcar after railcar, until the cyclops eye of the engine began to grow smaller and smaller in Red's sideview mirror.

About a half mile further down, the crossing came into view. The lights on the overhead panel commenced to flashing red, though the gate arm had not yet lowered. Red took hold of the door grip and pressed his feet to the floorboard.

Just as the barrier began to drop, Ezra punched the gas and they sailed through. Ezra let out a whoop, slapped at the steering wheel.

"Jesus Christ, kid," Red said through his teeth. "I didn't set out to play *Dukes of Hazzard*."

Ezra laughed. "It's cool Mr. Miller," he said. "If it'd been close, I never would have done it. I'm stupid, not crazy."

Red rolled his window down some to let the cooler evening air rush in, feeling his heart knocking through this shirt.

"That's a nice spot to eat," Ezra said randomly, pointing out the window. A small building sat a short distance back from the road, surrounded by a neatly manicured lawn, almost like an old carriage house. A half dozen or so cars were edged up to the entrance, mostly sedans. There was a brass nameplate against a line of shrubs, which Red couldn't't clearly make out. Something Manor.

"If you're ever looking for something a little fancy," Ezra said. "Cloth napkins and candles. That kind of place."

"Maybe another time," Red said, knowing full well there would not be another time.

The rest of the journey was a nonstop litany of stories about Ezra's high school baseball years, and all the glory you could imagine something like that might bring a young, good-looking fellow. He'd been so talented that he found himself on a farm team for the Cardinals. He lasted less than two months, until he blew out his elbow on the mound, somewhere in Iowa.

Before long, they were back at The Top Hat.

"Well, here we are," Ezra said. He reached his hand out. Red took it, gave it a good shake.

"I appreciate everything, son."

"You're welcome," Ezra answered. "I do hope you find Gina and that she and Noah are okay."

Red climbed out and watched as Ezra's truck pulled out onto the road. Once he was gone, he took the slow walk past the dozen or so rooms to his own. There were windows lit up and windows dark, drapes pulled tight. Near the end, the glow of the chili lights spilled out onto the walkway. A figure was seated in a chair just outside the room. As Red got closer, he could see that it was Morris. An accompanying cloud of cigar smoke lingered.

"Good evening, Morris," Red said as he came up on him. On the old man's knee, an ashtray was precariously balanced, the stub of a slender cigar smoldering in the center. Morris looked up at Red with a smile, but no obvious recognition.

"Are you the manager?" he asked.

"I'm your neighbor," Red replied. "The name's Red. Like

the color."

"Oh right," Morris said. "We met once before." He picked up the cigar and sucked on the end for a moment, then set it back down. He motioned with his hand toward the room behind him. "She's getting things ready for bed."

"You mean Sadie." Red craned his neck to peer inside the room, where Sadie was folding the covers down on one of the beds. She gave him a quick wave.

"She's a nice gal," Morris said. "You got any kids?"

"Yes sir. I have a daughter."

Morris leaned forward on his chair and looked down the walkway behind Red, then the other way. Red told him she wasn't there with him.

"What's she like?" he asked. "Your daughter."

"Oh well," Red said, reaching up and scratching his head as if Morris had asked a particularly hard question. "She's smart," he said finally. "Beautiful. She'll break your heart, though."

"Kids do that, but you gotta love 'em, right?" Morris turned in his seat and looked into his room. "The gal. Over there."

"Sadie." Red said again.

Morris gave a smile, with maybe a bit of recognition in it. "Sadie," he echoed. "That's the name of my daughter."

"Okay you two, party's over," Sadie called from inside the room. "Dad, put that smelly thing out and come on to bed."

Red sat on the edge of the bed in his room, counting through his remaining cash and cradling the phone against his neck. "She's waiting for the call," he said to the operator, as if the woman cared the least bit.

"Certainly," she said, and then a single ring later, there was Linda.

"Tell me you're okay!" Her voice shook, and that broke Red's heart.

"I'm okay, honey," he said. "I'm sorry I didn't call back right away. Me and Ezra had to go right away. Junebug..." He started with the rhubarb farm and Titus, and the bits about his rough treatment of Noah.

"I don't like hearing about someone being harsh with that little boy," Linda said. "What's this about a June bug? That's what you said, right?"

"Junebug," he went on. "She's this old gal who runs a kind of boarding house a few miles outside of town. Gina was living there up until the crash. She and Noah." He told her about Junebug chasing off Titus, and about Gina's bedroom, and the sobriety chip.

"Well now, that's a good thing, isn't it?"

"It's not a bad thing," Red answered. "It doesn't mean she's sober now, but it means she was sober once." And for the first time in as long as he could remember, he felt a little bounce of hope. Gina had been in a spot where she had finally accepted that things were wrong and that she was the one that had to change those things to make them right. For all those years, everything had always been someone else's fault. Teachers, cops. Red. Now, he dared to dream that things could be different.

Linda said suddenly, "Tell me more about the hair salon. How did you get a line on that?"

"There was a punch card among her stuff with all her appointments."

"How many punches were on it?"

Red reached into his wallet and took out the card. Seven out of ten stars were punched.

Linda was quiet for a moment, then remarked, "And the gal

there said she didn't know her."

"She remembered her, but didn't know much about her."

"Bullshit," Linda said. And before Red could ask where that was coming from, she said, "I'm coming out."

"No, no," he started. "You don't need…"

"Don't argue with me, Red," she snapped. "I've got the vacation days. There's no reason for me to be sitting here doing nothing. If I'm gonna twiddle my thumbs, let me do it where I can be of some support." She paused, giving him a few seconds to try and interrupt her. He held himself in, listening to the sound of her breathing from the other side of the mountains.

"If you want," he finally said. And when she was still silent, he added, "I would like it if you were here with me."

"That settles it," she said. "And the first thing we're gonna do is stop into this hair salon of yours."

# 13

It was a Sunday afternoon, and Red's father was up on the roof fiddling with the TV antenna and cussing at whoever might happen to hear. In the living room, the Philco sat on its stand, occasional flashes of images managing to break through the gray and white static. Red sat at the kitchen table, carefully stacking playing cards into a growing tower, while his mother stood by the sink peeling potatoes into a dented aluminum bowl. He was eleven, maybe twelve.

He remembered the shape of the talk, if not every word. At first, she let the scrape of metal and the dull tapping of the skins hitting the sides of the basin do the work. There was a rhythm there, and Red found himself following it, like tracing the noise trying to come from the TV. But then she suddenly said, "I almost left him once, you know." Just like that. No build-up. No warning.

Red didn't look over at her. He held the next card in his hand.

"He drank a lot back then," she said.

"He drinks a lot now," Red said to her.

"Well, it was worse then," she clarified. "You probably don't remember." Her voice wasn't angry or sharp, but was simply tired in that way adults get when so many of their decisions seem to land in the wrong place.

Red set the card down gently on top of the pile. The cards beneath it shifted just slightly, but held.

"I went so far as to packing a suitcase," she said. "Laid out my good shoes and your Sunday clothes. I had the Greyhound schedule taped inside the pantry door, where I knew he'd never see it." She stopped peeling the potatoes and stood there, one hip cocked against the counter, paring knife idle in her hand.

"Where would we have gone?" Red asked.

She didn't answer right away. She looked out the window instead, through the maple branches, toward the line of pickets that separated them from Mr. and Mrs. Garrity's yard. The breeze pushed through the leaves just enough to make a flurry of shadows dance over her face.

"I thought about heading south, then over to the ocean. My cousin had a place in Astoria. It was small, but there was a basement that was mostly dry. She said we could stay as long as we needed."

Red didn't know where Astoria was exactly, but he imagined it had blue skies and a beach and pipes that didn't break in winter. He wondered what it would be like to live someplace where people talked without yelling.

"But you didn't leave," he said, picking up another card.

"No, I didn't." Her voice folded in on itself then. She reached up and turned on the faucet, running the bowl under the water.

"How come?"

She let the paring knife drop into the sink. It clanged off the side, loud enough to make him jump. His fingers tapped an adjacent triangle and the cards slipped, falling flat onto the structure beneath it. Thankfully, the damage was minimal.

She wiped her hands on a dish towel, walked over to the

table and sat down across from him. Leaning-in close, she leveled her eyes with his. "Because leaving isn't just about packing a bag, honey. It's loading up everything—including all the things you can't possibly carry. Memories, guilt. All the advice you never took. I didn't think I could carry it all. Definitely not with you on my heels."

Red slid back in his chair, hard enough that the card tower trembled. The steeples on the top fell first, followed by a full collapse. All the work he'd done since coming home from church was sitting there in a scatter of red and black.

"Nuts," he said.

Outside, his father was yelling.

His mother brushed a hand over his hair. "Well, you were going to have to break it down anyway."

Red crawled out from under the covers and threw on his trousers and undershirt before heading outside. The lights over the pool were off, though there were a few spots of dim landscape fixtures positioned around the perimeter to indicate where the deck ended and the water began. By now, most all the windows along the walkway were dark. With the exception of the occasional rush of a passing car, it seemed like the whole world, except for him, was asleep.

He fumbled with some coins in his hand and pulled on the lobby door, the sharp ring of the bell prompting the desk gal to look up at him from a stack of books she had splayed out in front of her.

"Good evening, sir" she said. "Can I help with something?"

"Just looking for a midnight snack," he said, nodding to the pair of vending machines against the wall. "Figured I'd see what might be on the menu."

"Knock yourself out," she said. She rubbed at her eyes, and pulled an open book in front of her, the pages cluttered with diagrams and graphs. Taking a yellow highlighting pen in her hand, she raked it across the page, leaving a neon-colored stripe in its wake.

"Homework?" Red asked, dropping a couple of quarters into the slot and settling on a root beer. The can knocked its way on down.

"Always."

She was young and pretty, with shoulder length hair that was pinned back from her face with a couple of blue clips just above the ears. Red wondered if her parents knew that their daughter was working nights at a motel like this and if so, did they worry about her. Even though so far things had seemed fairly quiet at The Top Hat, Red had been around long enough to know that quiet could turn to racket pretty quickly.

"What are you studying?" he asked.

"This one's calculus," she said, folding the cover down so he could see it. "Math."

"Good grief," Red said, shaking his head. "What's all that lead to?"

"A headache to start," she said. "I'm hoping it ends with an engineering degree. Someday." She stretched her arms over her head and shut her eyes, tightening her muscles in the midst of a heavy yawn. "I got another year to go at North Idaho Community then I'm hoping to transfer down to the university. It's taking me twice as long as it should, though. Between work and money and life."

Red picked through the last of his change and emptied it into the candy machine, pulling the knob for a Hershey bar. "Those things always seem to find a way to complicate things," he said. "Work, money and life, that is."

"Whatever I need to do to get out of this place, I'll do, even if it takes me till I'm forty."

He gave her a thumbs up and went to the door, knocking the bell again as he swung it open. He paused before stepping out. "I'd be willing to bet that most roads in this town lead to somewhere else," he said. "When the time comes, all you've got to do is pick one and start driving."

He let the door shut behind him and popped the soda can top, taking a good drink as he made his way down the walkway to his room. The muffled sound of a television drifted from one of the blue-lit windows, tires screeching and gunshots tapping, and as he passed by, he heard a cough from over near the pool. He looked through the haze of the perimeter lights and saw a figure curled up on one of the patio recliners. As he drew nearer, he could see that it was Sadie. She was wrapped in a blanket and when she looked up at him, she pulled her arm from under the cover and brushed a hand over her face.

"Is everything all right?" he called out.

"Yeah," she answered, not sounding all right at all. She cleared her throat and wiped at her nose with her sleeve. "Let's just say it has been a day."

"A bad one, from the sounds of it."

"I guess. Not any worse than most days, to be honest. Just kind of caught up with me, you know?"

He walked over and sat next to her, tearing at the Hershey bar wrapper and breaking free a row of squares. "Here," he offered. "It won't fix everything, but I find that it can help."

"I'm just so tired," she said, taking the chocolate from him. "We went to a park about a mile from here," she explained. "I thought it'd be good to get out and see more of what's around us." She shook her head. "He shit himself, to be blunt. Didn't tell me he had to go until it was too late. We were probably fifty yards from the bathrooms and there was just no way it wasn't gonna happen. Of course he got upset, and I got upset, too. I yelled at him, 'I guess we're officially at the point of diapers.' People stared."

"Don't be hard on yourself," Red said. "It was a moment. We all get them."

"Oh, it was a moment all right," she laughed. She took the ends of the blanket and pulled it over the top of her head, so it looked like she was wearing a nun's habit. "There was a stretch of time," she said, "where I convinced myself that he—in the mind and body that is Morris right now —could bring out the best in me. We'd found ways to laugh again. I could sit with him and we could talk like old friends, and I didn't have to suffer that feeling like I used to, waiting for the cuts and the disappointments. Today was a sucker punch to all of that, because he definitely brought out the very worst in me." She sighed deeply. "And the funny thing about it all is that in that moment, I realized I was Morris. The Morris from thirty years ago, all teeth and eyes and loud. And I guess you'd have to say that he was me, wasn't he? The helpless, petulant little kid shitting her pants and making everything everyone was trying to do ten times harder than it ought to be." She shrugged her shoulder and took another bite of the chocolate. "I don't know," she said. "If nothing else it just validates that I made the right choice in not ever having kids. Thank God or Buddha or whoever for that."

Red didn't say anything to that. He handed her the bar and let her break off another row, and watched as she nibbled on the edge. It was hard to imagine her carrying on like she said she had, but he understood that people had that side of themselves, waiting to come out.

"Me and Gretchen," Red began. "My wife—my late wife—we probably had no business having a kid. We'd met later in life. Never expected that kids were even an option, so we never gave it much thought. Gina was a mistake, really."

"Unplanned," Sadie corrected. "My mother always said I was unplanned. Morris, he's the one who used the word 'mistake.'"

"Unplanned," Red repeated. "An unplanned surprise."

"There you go," she said, raising the last of her chocolate like it was a glass.

"I have this drawer in my kitchen," Red went on. "You probably do, too. Everybody's got one. The drawer where everything goes—stray screws, receipts, paper clips, glue. All kinds of shit. Shit you should go through and thin out, but you never do."

"I got five of 'em," Sadie laughed.

Red smiled. "Anyway, whenever I need some random thing, I go there first and dig around, always cussing at all the crap that's in there. If I get lucky, I'll find what I'm looking for, and I'm vindicated."

Sadie leaned forward.

"That is what it was like for Gretchen and me," he said. "Something would come up with Gina and, hell, we didn't know what to do. So, we'd run to the junk drawer in our heads. The one filled with all the things that our own parents ever did with us. Did to us, I guess, is a better way of putting it. And if we were lucky, we might find that one thing that actually worked. More times than not, though, everything we turned up was useless and so we had no choice but to wing it."

"If you can't find the screwdriver you use the butter knife," Sadie said.

"If you can find it." Red leaned back in his chair and folded his hands atop his head. "And if you can't find anything to show you how to deal with a kid knocking over a stack of soup cans at the grocery store and screaming herself blue—something that doesn't involve an ass-whooping, anyway—then what do you do?"

Sadie cocked her head to the side, as if she was processing the right answer to his question. "I just know that you don't yell at the top of your lungs that it looks like it's time for diapers."

# 14

Red came home from work, and there was Gina in front of the television, legs crossed, eyes glued to the screen.

"Whatcha watching?" he asked, but she didn't answer. "Mom around somewhere?" Gina just shrugged her shoulders.

Suddenly, there was the sound of water, of someone splashing, just like Gina would do when she played with her plastic fish and boats in the bathtub. Except Gina was on the carpet in the living room. Red ran down the hallway that was much longer than he remembered it to be, and began to pound on the bathroom door.

The splashing grew louder, and Red threw himself against the door, which fell open. There was Gretchen, sitting up in the tub, her smile and her eyes, and her beautiful body. She gave him a look that suggested he'd interrupted something, but that she didn't mind. But there was the splashing sound again, and Gretchen reached out her hand to him, as if she wanted him to join her in the water. He turned to close the door, afraid to look at her. Afraid that if he did, she would not be as she was right then, but rather how she had been that day—below the surface, her eyes gazing up at him, but not seeing anything.

He woke with the bed sheets soaked beneath him, cold to the touch. The dim light of early morning came through the edges of the curtains. There was the splashing sound again, outside his door this time. The pool.

"Those damned kids," Red said to himself. Except it was too quiet for them, too early.

He got up and went to the window and pulled the drapes aside. At the far side of the pool, a figure drifted and bobbed in the water, arms sweeping one way then the other, overhead and down with a dunking sound, white hair swept over a face that looked to have no earthly idea how or why he was where he was.

Morris.

Red ran out of his room and threw himself into the water, boxers, T-shirt and all, and in seconds he had Morris in his embrace. The old man gave a shout, as if Red had done something to hurt him. Red hoisted him up and paddled the two of them to the shallow end, where he was able to use his feet, dragging the old man up the low steps onto the deck. Morris sucked in a good breath through his confusion, his mouth moving like a hooked fish.

"Dad!" Here was Sadie now, rushing from her room, in a sweatshirt and jeans. Red wondered for a quick moment if she had slept in those clothes or if she had taken the time to get dressed before responding to her father.

"Oh my god, thank you," she said, her breath cutting into her words.

"Where the hell were you?" Red snapped.

"I'm sorry, what?" Her face changed in a snap. Her eyes became wide and fiery.

Red met her glare, and found himself wanting to take her hand and force it upon her father's, so that she might appreciate that he was still there with her.

Then her eyes began to well up, and Red had this overwhelming sense that he might as well have struck her with his fists. She stepped back from the edge of the pool, her knees bent and shaking. Along the walkway, a few windows had come to life, drapes pulled aside and faces peering out in the darkness, watching the whole scene. Red the savior, he imagined. Red the bully, he knew.

"I'm sorry," he sputtered. "I didn't mean…" He gently set Morris down in a chair and stepped quickly back from them both, his clothes soaked and hanging from his body in sheets, leaving a path of water behind him as he stumbled back to his room.

It was nearly six in the morning and Red found himself sitting on the edge of his bed. The damp sheets, along with his soaked shorts and T-shirt, lay piled in a heap against the wall. Though he'd laid every towel he could find over the mattress and changed into dry clothes, the idea of going back to sleep was about as realistic as Gina walking through the door.

Red went to the window and gazed outside. The pool surface was still and calm, as if nothing had happened. Sadie was sitting one of the lounge chairs, the blue haze of cigarette smoke lingering around her like a cloud.

He opened the door and went over to her without so much as a word. She sat there with her head down, as if she were studying the chipped, red polish on the toes of her bare feet.

He cleared his throat. She waved him off with the same hand that pinched the smoldering cigarette.

"You don't need to say it," she said.

"Again, I'm sorry," he said anyway.

She shook her head. "I fucked up," she said. "I pulled the goddamned bell from the door earlier and forgot to put it back up."

"People make mistakes."

"It could've been a hell of a lot more than a mistake," she said. "If it hadn't been for you…" Her words cut off, and she wiped at her eyes with the palm of her hand.

Red took a seat on the lounge beside her. "I had no business coming at you like I did," he said.

"It's okay."

"It's not okay," he insisted. He paused, ran his hand over his face. "We do the best we can. Go through life taking what we think are all the right roads in front of us. But sometimes we turn right when we're supposed to go left."

She looked up at him, the shadow of a landscape stretched across her forehead.

"Gina's mother," he said plainly. "She was in the bathtub. With a near empty bottle of bourbon on the floor next to her. Gina was in the living room when it happened." He caught his breath, his throat almost closing itself up when he said it. "I'm afraid I didn't handle it any better with Gina than I did with you."

"You were in shock." Sadie said. "Your daughter's old enough now to understand that. I'm sure she'd say the same."

While he appreciated that, it was nothing he hadn't heard many times before. He was allowed to react any way his emotions took him, everyone had told him. No matter how ugly it might have been, he'd somehow been given a free pass to tear away at the world around him. From everyone, that is, except Gina.

"I don't know," he said. "Anyway, I'm sorry for talking to you like I did."

"You know, if I can sit here in this fake Mexican vacation, after all the shitty things that man ever said or did to me over the years..." She reached into her pocket and took a pack of cigarettes, sliding a single one from the box. "I'm sure that whatever it was you said to her—in what had to be the worst moment of your life—she can find it in her heart to cut you a little slack."

# 15

Sunlight fell through the open drapes, waking Red from a deep sleep. It was warm in the room now; he had kicked the top blanket from his body so that it tangled, snakelike, around his feet. The nightstand clock read 9:17.

He got up and got dressed. Outside, the ringing of birdsong scattered over the noise of a nearby Hoover, its hum rolling back and forth against the wall. It dawned on Red that the noise was coming from Sadie and Morris' room.

He raked his hand through his hair and went out into the morning sun. The door to the room next door was wide open, the housekeeping cart positioned squarely in front. Inside, the vacuum buzzed, the figure of a woman—not Sadie—moving around the perimeter of the beds.

The pool surface was still and glassy, and all but one of the rooms along the walkway had its drapes open to the day. Red went back to his room, but before entering, noticed something affixed to the wooden frame outside his door, a piece of paper folded and pushed in place with a thumbtack. He pulled it free. It was one of those pre-printed message-memo things, with a note for him. He thought it might be from Sadie, or perhaps something from Linda. Maybe she was having second thoughts about the drive.

Deputy Brody was scrawled out at the top. Please stop by the station when you get a chance.

The station was busier than the last time Red had been there, with a half dozen or so folks milling around. An old couple sat on a hard wooden bench near the door, leg-to-leg, hands folded on their laps. The woman had a landscape of worry on her face, her mouth pinched at the edges, with layers of lines stretched across her forehead. The man gazed off into the distance, his eyes ticking from one police officer to the another.

Deputy Brody appeared from the conference room and gave a wave to Red to come on back.

"I'm assuming you're still playing detective," he said as Red took a seat. "Considering you're still at the motel."

"You're assuming correct," Red answered. He didn't mention Junebug, as he didn't want to do anything to put her in Brody's crosshairs.

Brody took the chair opposite Red and laid the familiar manila envelope between them. "I can't say I've fared any better," he said. "But I have come into some information that I thought you might want to know about."

Red leaned in and placed his elbows on the table.

"It's about the night she went missing," Brody began. "The night of the crash."

The night of the crash.

"There's a place up north on the way to Sandpoint," Brody continued. "A big blueberry farm run by a fellow by the name of Quay. In addition to blueberries, Quay also, on occasion, hosts a cockfight ring in a big, red barn set up on a hill."

"I thought cockfights were illegal," Red commented.

"They are." The deputy tipped back in his chair. "I said 'on occasion.' It's one of those things that we get word about after the fact, and not often enough for us to sit there and watch for day in and day out."

"Fair enough."

Brody went on. "According to what I have, Gina and her fellow Titus showed up at the fights a little past 10:30 p.m. Gina stayed in the car, while Titus went in and made a hundred dollar bet on the next pair of roosters. Now, if you've never been to something like this, as soon as the roosters get going, all hell breaks loose with those who are placing bets. It can be pandemonium, and it sounds like Titus knew that, because somehow he got himself close enough to the cash bag to grab it and run." Brody paused, eyeballing Red for a moment. "So, he hauls ass down the hill to where Gina's waiting, and by the time anyone figures out what the hell is happening he's already a good fifty yards ahead of them. One witness I talked to says that when Titus got to the car, he started hollering at Gina. A few seconds later she starts up the car, puts it into gear and they tear on out of there."

Red let all this settle for a moment, picturing what Brody had just laid out for him. Then he told the deputy that if Gina had been a part of this thing from the beginning, the engine would have already been running: "There wouldn't have been any yelling. If she knew what he was up to ahead of time, she'd have been ready."

"Possibly," Brody acknowledged. "Bottom line is, with Titus in the morgue and Gina gone—and nothing of interest turned up at the crash site—the overarching question is where the money ended up."

"Did you already talk to this Quay fellow?" Red asked.

"Yep. He played dumb, of course. Danced around the cockfighting thing, downplayed the stolen money. Said it wasn't enough to make a federal case out of. That it sounded like the windshield did a hell of a lot more to Titus Riggs than he'd ever have done."

"But you don't believe him?"

Brody shrugged his shoulders. "It's hard to say, to be honest. Officially, he's let it go since the stolen money was gotten by illegal means. I can't say he's not looking for Gina like we are. Five grand or thereabouts isn't chump change. Let me just say that it'd likely be a bad day for her if she crossed in front of his pickup in the middle of Main Street."

When Red got back to The Top Hat, Linda's Fastback was already there in the parking lot, pulled up neatly into a stall near the office. Since it was barely noon, she had to have left her place well before dawn. He parked next to her, scanning the inside of her car before peeking inside the office at the empty chairs.

Turned out she was on the pool deck, stretched out on a lounger with her suitcase at her side, already in cutoffs and a T-shirt.

"It's good to see you in one piece," she said.

"It's good to see you in any way, shape or form," he smiled.

"I'm not sure what that says about what you're seeing," she said with a tilt of her head. "I'll take it as a compliment, though."

He went to her, gave her a quick kiss and took the seat next to her, placing his hand in hers. "You can take a dip if you want," he said, motioning to the water.

"I didn't bring a suit."

"What you're wearing is fine," he said. "This ain't the Holiday Inn."

She laughed at that, told him that from what she'd already seen, she could safely admit that she'd stayed in a lot worse places. She gave his hand a squeeze.

"Did they have anything new?" she asked. "The sheriff I mean."

"Yes and no." He let go of her hand and leaned back on the lounger. He told her about the cockfight, and the money. And when she said, "Oh, that doesn't sound good," he replied, "No it sure doesn't." He also let her on about what had happened with Morris and the pool last night, but left out his yelling at Sadie and the dream about Gretchen.

"I tell you what," he said. "I could go for some breakfast."

"Red Miller," Linda said, "you've read my mind."

They sat in a booth, the window facing southwest, the high sun pressing down on the table like a campfire. Linda was halfway through her steak and eggs, not having mentioned Gina once since the two of them left the motel. Her silence, however, didn't mean that she had nothing to say.

"How is it?" Red asked.

"It came from a cow." She worked the fork along the edge, cut a bite and handed it across the table. Red took it from her and popped it into his mouth, the meat dry and leathery. Linda took the fork back and set it down gently on her plate. Leaning her elbows on the table, she looked Red square in the eye. The edges of her mouth curled ever so slightly, like tiny parenthesis on either side of her lips. She said nothing, just stared at him as if he was in the middle of a long, drawn-out story that she was hanging on every word of.

"So," he said, knowing what she was thinking. "Gina."

"Gina." She shook her head from side to side. "I was thinking," she said, "On the drive over here..."

"There's time and distance for that."

"I was wondering about that beautician you talked about seeing."

"What about her?" Red asked. "She didn't know anything."

"The card, though. Do you have it on you?"

Red took his wallet from his back pocket and fished out the card. If she wanted to see it, he didn't have any objection. It wasn't like there was going to be a confession written on there that he'd missed.

Linda took him, turned it over in her hand. "Yeah, it's what I figured," she said, handing the card back.

"What of it?" He looked at the card. Punched holes and scribbles.

"If you look at the dates on those punches, they're roughly a month apart."

"Okay?" Red answered, puzzled.

"So, Gina's been going to this gal every month for the last six months at least. And you can bet there's been cards before this one. You don't have a standing monthly appointment with someone for god knows how long and then have to search your brain to try and remember them. I'd bet my Volkswagen that gal isn't being straight with you."

"You think she's lying?"

"I think she's not giving you the full story," Linda said. "For whatever reason."

"You want to drive by there?" he asked.

"Even more," Linda said with a wink, "I insist on it."

They pulled into the gravel lot, and Red brought his truck to a stop just shy of the yellow painted parking block. The sun was high now, and directly behind them, hitting the front windows and door of the salon with a glare that Red couldn't see through. "I wonder if she's here," he said, glancing up and down the strip. The El Camino wasn't anywhere in sight.

"Well, we won't know until we're inside, right?" Linda reached up and pulled the handle of her door, stepping down onto the running board. The smell of hot concrete and road dust tumbled in.

The receptionist looked up at them when they came in, the same gal, Karla, who'd spent Red's last visit as a prisoner to the telephone. Thankfully, she didn't seem to recognize him. In the middle chair behind her, a woman who was not Rosie raked a comb through the hair of a client, a woman a bit older than Red, dark hair with just the hint of gray to lay a stripe down her head. The stylist took up a pair of scissors and clipped away, thin tufts of brown falling like leaves from her hands.

"By chance is Rosie around?" Red asked.

"Rosie doesn't work on Tuesdays," Karla said. She leaned forward against the counter, wrapping her arms over her chest as if she might have something to hide. "If you wanna wait, I could see if Sandy could squeeze you in for a haircut."

"It's for me," Linda interrupted. "I'm pretty sure we had an appointment." She glanced quickly at Red. "Rosie and me." She reached into her pocket and took out the punch card. "I'm working on a freebie."

Karla drew in her lower lip. "Rosie doesn't work on Tuesdays," she repeated. She then reached over to a stack of papers on the edge of the desk and pulled out a notebook. Flipping it open, she thumbed through the first page, then turned a few more, running her finger from top to bottom. "What did you say your name was?" she asked.

"Tammy," Linda said, shooting a look at Red again. "With a 'Y'."

Karla went from page to page. "I'm not seeing anything. Are you sure it was Rosie?"

"Who else works here?" Linda asked.

"Besides Rosie, and Sandy there, we have Star and Cheryl."

"I don't think I'd mix those names up," Linda said. "Are any of them blond?"

"They all are." Karla motioned toward Sandy. "Except her."

Just then, the telephone rang.

"Is one of them kind of heavyset?" Linda asked. "A big girl?"

"Again," Karla smiled. "Pretty much…" She nodded over to Sandy again, then looked down at the phone as it continued ringing. "I need to…"

Linda motioned to the notebook on the desk. "I'm positive I set something up when I was in here last," she said. "Do you mind if I just take a quick glance?"

Karla shot a pointed look at Linda, then back at the insistent telephone. She picked up the notebook and handed it over, then answered the phone. "Curl Friends," she chirped. "Girl!," she squealed. She twirled in her chair so that she faced away from Red and Linda, cupping her hand over the mouthpiece. "Oh, you know," she said, then continued on with some bit of business neither one of them could make out.

Linda leaned on the counter and turned the pages in the notebook, whispering to herself as she did so—whatever the heck she was saying, Red couldn't make it out.

"Can I help you?" It was Sandy. She stood there, frozen in place, a clump of hair in her fist. "That's not really for the public to go through. People's names and stuff."

Linda looked up. "Definitely lots of names," she said,

"I honestly don't know what happened; I'm sure I had an appointment with Rosie." With that, she closed the notebook. "Clearly she doesn't work on Tuesdays."

Red lit out onto the highway and headed north toward Rockview, while Linda fiddled with the ashtray clip on the console with her thumb. She seemed to rolling something over in her mind.

"She's a regular all right," she finally said. "Gina."

"Well, you saw her name in the book."

"Pretty much every month since the beginning of the year, some of them blocked out for a couple of hours. That's a full color set. And not just written down like it was nothing. Gina, all in loopy writing, with a star where the dot would be."

Red wondered what significance a star over Gina's name might have.

"You probably don't get where I'm going," Linda said, as if she'd read his mind. She reached up and, maybe unintentionally, maybe not, ran her fingers through her hair. "You told me before that when you went there and talked to Rosie that she acted like Gina's name and picture barely registered with her."

"That's true."

"She's lying her ass off, Red." Linda shook her head. "You don't have a standing appointment every month with the same hairdresser, especially in a small town, without earning the status of being a regular. You know what I mean?"

"I think so," Red said. "You probably don't put a star over someone's name if you don't know them very well."

"Unless you do it for everyone in the book, which she didn't."

Red gazed out at the field of fruit trees, which stretched from the highway's edge like an endless company of soldiers, each row clicking by in the blink of an eye. "So, we ought to swing back by there tomorrow, then," he said. "See if we can't get a straight answer out of her."

"We can try," Linda said. "I'd be willing to bet, though, that that hairdresser is probably on the phone with her right now, telling her that someone was looking for her." She started fiddling with the ashtray again, her thumb clicking the tab a few times.

The exit sign rose up over the low ridge coming into Rockview, a smattering of fast food, gas station and shop signs stretching into the distance.

They drove for a few blocks in silence, Linda seeming to take in the whole of the town as they did so. She had her hand on her chin as if committing the landscape to memory. As if she might need to find her way on her own at some point.

"Is that the feed store?" she asked, motioning to Red's left. "Where that kid works?"

Red looked at the sign peeking back at him between a pair of cypress trees. Rockview Farm and Feed.

"You mean Ezra," he said. "Yeah, that'd be it."

"Ezra," Linda echoed. "Do you think it might be good to stop by and see him?" She was looking over at Red with that smile of hers, like she had something up her sleeve that she wasn't ready to show just yet.

"I don't know that he'll have anything more for us."

"I'd be curious to see if he has anything to say about our stylist Rosie," she pressed. "Gina was probably getting her hair done back when he was in the picture, don't you think?"

Red considered this and let his breath out in a heavy sigh. He was glad to have Linda there with him, but she had a lot of ideas. It was almost like she'd been piecing in her head the whole time how he should be going about this.

At the next intersection he hooked a U-turn and doubled back to the feed store. He stopped close to the loading dock, rolled down his window and leaned out on his elbow. Several fellows had formed a relay line, passing heavy burlap bags of feed from one to the next. Ezra was right there in the middle of it all.

He glanced in Red's direction. He gave Ezra a nod, but then just as quick, the kid looked away, as if jerked by an invisible thread.

"We'll wait here for them to finish," Red told Linda. "It shouldn't be more than a minute or so."

The minute turned into five, and once the pallet was empty the fellows scattered. Only then did Ezra make his way over. He moved like his arms and legs were numb, head down, as if he was coming only out of obligation, or perhaps shame.

It was only when he got close that Red got a good look at his face. A wine-colored bloom spread under his left eye, just to the ridge of his cheekbone, and his lower lip was swollen a third of so of its normal size, like he'd been stung by a bee.

"Mister Miller," he said.

"Ezra." Red motioned to Linda. "This here is Linda Foss. She made the trip all the way out here to see if she couldn't help in the effort."

"Ma'am," Ezra said. "Pleasure to meet you."

"Likewise. You look like you took a tumble."

"You could say that." Ezra grinned, then looked to Red. "I don't want to be rude, Mr. Miller, but I'd prefer if you didn't come around here anymore. I don't have anything left to say about Gina."

Red turned briefly to Linda; the two of them locked eyes. "I got a little more info about her activities that night," he said to Ezra. "I wondered if you might've heard more since we last talked."

"Well, I haven't," Ezra said, shifting his weight from one foot to the other. The collar of his T-shirt was damp with sweat. He glanced past Red, in the direction of the road.

"Nothing?" Red pressed. "About the cockfight?"

Ezra's eyes clicked back to focus on Red, his fat lip trembling a bit. Finally, he said, "Nothing, sir."

Linda cleared her throat. "We don't want to make things hard for you," she said. "It's just that..." she paused, smiled. Then she turned back to Red. "We should go now. Let him get back to work before he gets into trouble."

Red looked up at the loading dock, to the shadows near the back of the warehouse. Several figures moved in the darkness, back and forth, almost like dancers. While he felt sure that this and that still lingered in Ezra's mind, Red had a pretty good sense that the injuries the kid was sporting had something—if not everything—to do with his poking around. "Sure," he said, "I appreciate your time and candor." He reached out and took the boy's hand. "I'll leave you be."

Ezra shook his hand back. "You have a nice day, ma'am," he mumbled to Linda. She stretched her arm out and patted his shoulder before turning and climbing back into the pickup truck.

And as Red went to do the same, Ezra said, "Sir?"

Red paused.

"I do hope you find her, I really do. I just can't be mixed up in this anymore. I hope you understand."

And he did. Understand. If he didn't before, he understood now the expectation of silence in a place like this, among people like these. The pull between what a person should do versus what they had to do. But he didn't say any of that to Ezra. Instead, he just shrugged his shoulders, climbed into the cab and fired up the engine—with a little more muscle than necessary—before steering out into the roadway, down the street back to the motel.

"I was thinking," Linda piped up.

"About what?"

"I was thinking I'd put on my cutoffs and borrow one of your shirts," she said. "Take a dip in the pool after all."

# El Camino

Red changed into a pair of Bermuda shorts, peeled off his shirt and stretched out on a lounger. He watched as Linda paddled herself on an inflatable from one end of the pool to the other. Now and then, she directed herself to the edge of the pool for a sip of Coke and a handful of the corn chips Red had bought from the vending machine. It was nice to just be there, the two of them, not chasing possibilities and details all over the Idaho panhandle.

"So, what happened with your friend?" Linda asked.

"Which friend is that?"

"The neighbor. The old man and Mexico."

Red caught himself smiling. "Those two," he said. "You just missed them. They checked out today."

Linda popped the last few chips into her mouth. The shadow of a deck umbrella fell over her. "That's a shame," she said. "They sounded like quite the pair. I'd have liked to have met them."

"You'd have gotten a kick out of them for sure." A sliver of sunlight poked out over the corner of the umbrella, temporarily blinding him. Even with the sun in his eyes, he could feel Linda's gaze. She must know there was more that he wasn't saying.

"It got ugly there at the end," he admitted, adjusting the umbrella so that it blocked out the sun.

Linda sat up on the inflatable, letting her legs fall on either side, holding herself in place with her hand on the deck. "How ugly?" she asked.

He told her about Morris in the pool, and the scolding he'd given Sadie. When Linda said, Oh, and nothing further, he explained how it had been Morris' splashing that had woken him up from his dream about Gretchen, and the bathtub. "You know about that," he said. He sat up in the lounger and folded his hands between his knees and pressed them together. "About how she drowned."

"I know that she drowned in the tub," Linda said. "You've never told me how."

"I was at work," he started, feeling a lightness in his head and chest. "Gretchen was at home, like always. I told you she was a housewife. Even after Gina started school, it was what she wanted."

"It's not an unusual thing," Linda said.

"She acted like she was happy, and I think most of the time she really was. There was some volunteer stuff once in a while. Things at Gina's school. But as time went on, she started staying at home more and more..." He paused.

"And then?"

"And then?" He took a deep breath. "That's when it seemed like her drinking started to pick up. Not a whole bunch, at least not at first. There would be times I'd see her after work and catch a whiff of it on her breath. Or she might pick me up and I'd notice she seemed a bit off. Kind of high or something. As much as it unsettled me, I didn't say anything, at least not directly. I never really knew how to approach it. It didn't seem like a big enough problem. She was still Gretchen, at least most of the time." He looked away from Linda and the pool, tracing the top of a concrete wall separating the pool deck from the street. Patches of weeds had taken root on top of the wall.

"I'd been standing in the rain after my shift was done, waiting for her and Gina," he continued. "Gretchen had a couple things she wanted to do that day, so I let her have the truck. It had been a while since there were any issues, so I thought it'd be okay."

Linda reached up and took hold of his foot.

"I don't remember how long it was," he went on, "but it got to where I was wondering just where the hell they were. I called the house, but there was no answer."

And then the story suddenly flowed out of him like a busted spigot.

"I caught a ride with a buddy of mine...And when we got to the house, I could see the pickup was sitting right there in the driveway. I could also see that the TV was on...That damned TV." He ground his teeth, the sensation of fingernails raking his back "Gina was on the living room carpet with her eyes glued to the screen. I remember there was a variety show of some kind on. People dancing. Music...I asked her where her mother was and she just shrugged her shoulders. I asked if she'd seen her since she got home from school and she shook her head. Just kept staring at that goddamned TV like she was hypnotized."

The rest, he explained to Linda, was something of blur. He called out Gretchen's name, but there was no answer. As he walked from room to room, he remembered feeling his heart starting to pound harder and harder, and then he discovered the locked bathroom door.

"I pounded on it so hard," he told her. "I'm not even sure how, but all of a sudden the jamb was in splinters, the door hanging from the wall by a single hinge...Gretchen was lying there in the bathtub, her face maybe six inches below the surface of the water...She was like a ghost. The water was almost clear but not quite, like she was resting in a kind of haze. And those eyes of hers." He caught his breath, and held his hand to his mouth. "Her eyes were just staring up at the ceiling like she was looking at something only she could see."

He told Linda about how he pulled the body from the water, and how it was so icy and he couldn't imagine anything could be so cold. He didn't recall laying Gretchen down on the floor, or how he got himself from the bathroom to the living room. But he vividly remembered stomping over to the television and kicking it so hard that it slid across the floor into the wall, the screen flashing white before going dark and silent. And the smell that came from the smallest puff of smoke—sharp and acidic.

"I had no business," he said, shaking his head.

"Oh honey," Linda reassured him. "You'd just found your wife's body. You had to have been out of your mind with grief."

"I remember the look on her face," Red said. "Gina's face. She was so confused. One minute she was in her own little world of whatever, and the next the box is on the other side of the room and her father is standing over her, asking her where the hell she thought her mother had been the last three hours."

Red stopped, and slid back in the lounger. Linda reached over and rested her hand against his calf, giving it a gentle squeeze as if he were a child.

"If there was any hope for Gina," he went on, "I sure as hell crushed it right then. I mean, what could she have done? Eight years old? And anyway, the EMTs figured Gretchen been gone at least an hour before Gina even stepped off the bus. Even if she'd have thought to call someone, it wouldn't have mattered." He looked up at the sky, at a wisp of clouds that stretched overhead like the dance of bedsheets on a clothesline. It all seemed like a separate life that happened so long ago, even as fresh as everything felt in the telling. Gina had been so young, her bed unmade as always, toys scattered around her room. Two plates at the table after Gretchen was gone, no way for her to know what might come tumbling out of his mouth. Maybe now, he thought, with the responsibilities of motherhood, she could finally understand that sometimes the best of intentions bring about the worst of outcomes.

They sat there silently together for a good while, holding onto one another as if their lives depended upon it. An easy breeze picked up, cooling Red's naked skin. Linda gave his stomach a gentle rub.

"I'd guess I'm about a half shade from being full lobster red," she said, breaking the silence.

"More pink lemonade," he said. "You'll be okay." And then, moving the train of conversation like a last-minute railroad switch, he asked, "Have you thought about dinner?" The sun had begun to dip behind the trees and the dappled light on the water bled to orange.

"Not really," she claimed. "But I suppose I could eat something by the time we settle on a place. Someplace quiet, maybe."

"Cloth napkins?" he asked. "Candle on the table?"

"Well, in that case," she smiled, "Red Miller, you know how I think."

The two of them walked hand in hand to the motel office where they found the gal who had been studying calculus staring down at a paperback copy of *Catch-22*.

"That's a heavy read," Linda said to her. The girl didn't answer, turning a page.

"For a class, I'm guessing," Red added.

"For me," she replied. She dog-eared the page, setting the book on the table in front of her. "Would you like to check out?"

"I hope not," Linda said. "I just got here."

"We're looking for a place to get a good steak," Red said.

"Patty's Diner makes good steaks," she said. "It's down the road."

"Yeah, we had breakfast there," Linda said. "We were hoping for a place a step or two up."

With that, the gal pulled back in her chair and shot a look at Linda that was laced in defensiveness, as if maybe her mother or sister waited tables at Patty's. As if she'd caught her error, Linda added, "We loved the food there. We're just looking for something more..." She paused and looked over to Red.

"Someone told me about a place up north, Manor something-or-other.

"Devereaux Manor," the girl said. "It's pretty nice. You gotta wear a jacket, though."

"I have a jacket," Red confirmed.

"Yes, you do," Linda said with a gentle swipe of his arm.

The girl looked at the two of them, the faintest smile breaking through. "A sports jacket, right?"

"Yes ma'am," Linda said brightly.

The sun had fallen behind the western ridge, the temperature reliably following suit. Red's sports jacket hung on the hook in the cab behind his seat. Linda had grabbed a sweater, carrying it with her like it was a cat. She'd done up her makeup, and she wore a smile that was so solid that Red caught himself feeling bad that in all the time they'd been going together, he hadn't once taken her to the type of place that she needed to spruce up for. That it was happening for the first time amidst all this craziness was something.

"Here's the belle of the ball," he said, holding the passenger door for her like it was a limousine.

"Prince Charming," she quipped, hoisting herself into the seat and pulling the seatbelt over her lap. "Just don't keep me out past midnight."

He pulled out onto the main drag and gave the engine a little gas. Linda started fiddling with the radio dial, landing on a station halfway through a Patsy Cline song.

"I was in the hospital with my old man when the news came out that she was killed," Red said. He could see his father there in the bed, face gaunt and yellow as butter, cirrhosis eating up the last of his liver, as Red adjusted the antenna on a small radio on the nightstand. It had been a plane crash, on her way back to Nashville from a show she'd done in Kansas City. Red's father shook his head slowly, his lower lip quivering like a punished child. "I think it was the only time I'd ever seen him choked up like that."

"Red," Linda interrupted. "Is that an El Camino over there?" She pointed to a cluster of cars lined up at a service station. Pulled up aside a lone pump was one fine-looking '64 El Camino, black and glassy. Huddled at the rear quarter panel wasn't Rosie, but a man, thick-bodied and broad-shouldered, flannel shirt draped loose over blue jeans, balancing the pump handle like he was feeding a bottle to a baby. In the passenger seat, was the silhouette of what appeared to be a woman, though it was impossible to make out the face.

"I'll be damned," Red said. He let off the gas, the truck rolling to a crawl.

"What do you want to do?" Linda asked.

"I don't know. Probably wouldn't be good to ambush them," he joked.

"Probably not," Linda agreed.

Red steered off the road and onto the shoulder, bringing the pickup to a stop. He watched in the rearview as the fellow finished up with the pump, shaking it like he was standing at the toilet, then climbed into the driver's side. The brake lights winked a couple of times, followed by a puff of smoke from the tailpipe as the car pulled away from the station.

Neither of them said anything for a moment. Linda leaned forward in her seat, turning to look at Red. She reached her hand out to touch his, so lightly that he barely felt it.

"I guess we should head to dinner then," he said.

"Or not." She gave him a sharp rap on the knuckles. "Maybe we do a little pursuit. See where they're off to."

Red kept a safe distance behind the El Camino, snaking through town and out into the open county, transitioning onto a shoddy, pocked road that curled in what he surmised was a northerly direction. The cloudless sky was falling into a deep, almost slate blue hue. Shadows fell from the rows of apple trees in long, black stripes so that the landscape crisscrossed like a giant, tartan quilt. There were landmarks here and there that by now were familiar to Red. A faded billboard ad, pushing Jesus. A self-service car wash under a cinderblock canopy, surrounded by a field of waist-high weeds. Broken down barns and car farms, and the stretch of roadway cutting a slice through what felt like an endless plain.

It wasn't until they came up over the far crest that the trees seemed to reclaim the land, and an old roadhouse popped into view. A crusty old sign read SHORTY'S. Beer names winked from the neon-dressed windows. Red watched as the El Camino's brake lights blazed, and the car turned into the lot, a rooster tail of dust blooming behind it.

Red followed the El Camino into the lot, winding among the two dozen or so cars to take a spot under a big willow that stood alone near the back. He popped the stick into park and tapped the brake. "I don't know about this," he said to Linda.

"We're just sitting here," she replied.

Two figures got out of the El Camino but in the fading light, it was hard to get a good look at them.

"We don't need to say anything to them," Linda said. "Just go in and have a drink. Watch them a little bit. If it feels right, we can strike up a conversation. If not, we get out of Dodge."

Red opened his door and drew his leg out onto the running board, pausing for a moment to look back at Linda. It dawned on him that what he thought he knew about her and what she was actually capable of were two different things. Here was a woman who seemed to have no fear, driven hard enough by what was right to risk god-knows-what in her quest to fix what was broken.

Linda opened her door and climbed out of the car into the evening. Red locked up the rig and followed after her as she made a beeline for the El Camino. She paused at the driver's side door and peered inside.

"She is a beauty," Red said.

"Sure beats my Volkswagen," Linda agreed.

Red glanced over to the door of the roadhouse.

"What are you thinking?" Linda asked him.

"I'm thinking that I don't have the foggiest idea how I'm

gonna casually strike up a conversation with the guy," he said. "I didn't even get a decent enough look at him or the gal he's with. They could be anyone."

"But you're positive this is the same car?"

"Hundred percent."

"Well, all right then." And with that, Linda took his keys from him and walked back to the pickup truck and opened the door. She leaned inside, and emerged a few moments later holding something in her hand that Red couldn't quite make out. It wasn't until she was back beside him that he could see it was the coat hanger his jacket had been hanging from.

"What are you planning to do with that?" he asked.

"I want to have a look inside." She began to rotate the hook, twisting the hanger into a long, single rod. "I've done this a million times," she reassured him. But, as quickly as she had begun, she stopped and pressed on the handle. The unlocked door swung open.

"All that nonsense for nothing," she said, tossing the hanger into the bushes. She reached inside to the dash and pulled the headlamp knob. A vacant lot across the street, shin-high grass stretching from the fence line, lit up like a small ocean.

"Draining the battery? That's your plan?"

Linda flashed an impish grin, then walked ahead of him to the front door of the roadhouse, yanking it open and marching inside like she was a regular.

Several windows framed the front room; those that weren't crowded with neon signs had sheets of paper, newspaper clippings maybe, taped to the glass. The floor was littered with discarded peanut shells and cigarette butts. In one corner, a parquet dance floor lay empty and dark.

The crowd, such as it was, was clustered in booths or bellied up to the bar. A country western song that Red didn't recognize played on the jukebox. In a side room separated from the rest of the tavern by a set of saloon doors, the sound of pool balls knocking against one another occasionally pierced the music.

Linda went right over to the bar and said something to the bartender, a fellow that Red imagined could easily pick up work as a department store Santa Claus during the holidays.

The man gave Linda a nod, then walked to the end of the bar and reached under and fiddled with something. Just like that the music stopped, and he produced a palm-sized microphone.

"If you're driving a black El Camino," he crackled over the crowd, "your lights are on."

Linda leaned into Red. "Now watch."

Save for a few curious heads swiveling back and forth, no one moved at first. Finally, at a booth near the dance floor, a figure wearing a flannel shirt slid to the edge of his seat and stood up. He picked up a tall glass of beer, half empty already, and tipped it to his mouth, draining like it was a shot glass. He then cracked a peanut between his fingers and tossed the meat into his mouth, scattering the shells at his boots. Walking towards the front door, he moved through the bar like he'd been poured into it—shoulders loose, flannel shirt draped loose over his jeans. His mustache, thick and paintbrush-straight, jumped with each step he took.

"There's your guy," Linda said with a nudge of her elbow.

Red broke away from her and followed the man through the haze of smoke and chatter, out the door and into the cool night air. The man didn't look back, just walked steady to the far end of the lot where the El Camino sat glowing under a floodlight. He opened the driver's side door and clicked off the headlights.

"That's a nice ride you got there," Red called out.

"Yeah," the man said. "She's something, ain't she?"

"She yours?"

The man grinned, proud and easy. "Sure is. '64 El Camino. Two eighty-three cubic-inch V8, four-barrel carb."

"Dual exhaust?"

"Yes! She'll do two hundred and twenty horses if you treat her right."

Red whistled softly. "That's a clean setup. Most folks let 'em rot out before they even hit that mileage."

"Tell me about it," the man said, coming closer, his grin widening. "This one's a desert car. Dry all its life. I rode a Greyhound down to Reno to get her—buddy of mine won it in a poker game, called me up, said I could have it for a price that'd be a sin to turn down."

"Sometimes you gotta grab the brass ring when it comes around."

"Damn right."

They stood there a moment, both of them eyeing the car like it was a woman worth arguing over.

"I take it you're a car man?" the fellow asked.

"I am," Red said. "Backyard mechanic, mostly."

"You got that look. Somebody who knows a torque wrench from a tire iron."

Red chuckled under his breath.

"I ain't seen you here before," the man said.

"Me and my lady are just passing through."

"To where? There ain't a hell of a lot on either side of this thing they call a town."

"Here and there," Red said. "Sightseeing."

"There's plenty to see all right. Just not a lot that's worth writing down, if you get what I mean. But then it's not like I've lived here my whole life." The man stuck out his hand. "Name's Landry."

"Red."

Landry tipped his chin toward the front door of the tavern. "You buying or hiding?"

Red smiled. "Guess I could go for a round."

Back inside, Red spotted Linda waving at him from a booth across the room, right next to the one Landry had been sitting at. A fresh beer waited in the middle of the table.

Landry noticed her too. "That your lady?"

"Yeah."

"Pretty thing."

Just then, a gal who was sitting in Landry's booth turned toward them. She had curly hair and was wearing a denim jacket studded with rhinestones that winked each time she moved.

As if he'd read his mind, Landry said, "That's Ruby. She comes out with me sometimes. Don't know why." He grinned, looking over his shoulder at Red. "You'll like her. Everybody does." He lifted a hand and gave her a lazy wave, then headed over to her. Red followed.

"Red, this here's Ruby," Landry said. "Ruby, this is Red. He's traveling with his lady."

Linda got up from the next booth and stood beside Red.

"This is…" Red began.

"Caroline," Linda finished.

Caroline? Red thought, not knowing what to think.

Ruby offered a small, warm smile. "Caroline. Pretty name."

"Thank you," Linda said. "That's a nice jacket you've got."

Ruby smoothed a hand down the rhinestones. "Picked it up at a flea market down in Lewiston. Figure if I'm gonna live in a place with no sparkle, I might as well make some myself."

Linda laughed. "Can't argue with that."

"You'll find this town moves slow," Ruby said. "Folks mean well, but you'll learn everything there is to know about them in one afternoon. And they'll learn just as much about you by the next morning."

"She's right about that," Landry said. "Small-town radar. You can't sneeze without someone blessing you from three blocks over." He sat down beside Ruby and motioned for Linda and Red to sit down on the other side of the booth. A waitress came by, and Landry ordered a round for the table.

"You two just passing through?" he asked.

Linda spoke first. "Up from Sacramento. Taking in the scenery, maybe thinking about a change of pace."

"That right?" Landry said. "Funny—your fella here said you were sightseeing."

"Well," Linda said easily, "sometimes sightseeing turns into scouting."

Red gave a short laugh. "Guess we didn't get our story straight."

Landry chuckled. "Hell, most married folks can't agree on dinner, let alone direction."

The small talk drifted between them—cars, weather, road conditions on Highway 2. Landry asked Red a few questions about his work, about where they were headed next. Red dodged specifics. Linda filled the spaces with bright, harmless chatter.

When they had all finished their beers, Landry pointed toward the swinging doors in the back. "I have a feeling there's a pool table with our name on it."

Ruby gave him a look that mixed fondness and warning.

"He's just looking for somebody new to hustle."

Landry smiled. "Only if they're worth the lesson."

Red met his eye. "We'll see who ends up learning." He pushed off the booth and nodded toward the bar. "I'll grab a pitcher if you can wrangle us a table."

"Deal," Landry said. "Don't be long—I play better before the beer gets warm." He got up and weaved through the crowd until he passed through the swinging doors.

"That's the last we'll see of him for the rest of the night," Ruby sighed.

"I'm going to hit the ladies' room," Linda announced.

Ruby smiled faintly and shook her head. "Take your time. I'll hold down the fort."

Linda leaned close to Red as they made their way through the bar area.

"Caroline?" he murmured.

She smirked. "Felt like the right name."

Red shook his head. "You and your instincts."

"Don't start," she said. "He likes you."

"Maybe," Red said. "Or maybe he just likes being liked."

Landry set up the rack, then took it upon himself to do the break. He managed to sink the six, a lucky shot as far as Red could tell.

The game seesawed back and forth, Red dialing back what he was pretty good at, letting Landry stay a ball or two ahead. It came down to the end, Landry pointing his cue at the corner pocket, then sinking the eight ball to close it out.

"You ever play for coins?" Landry asked, dropping a quarter into the slot. There was a rumbling as the balls made their way down the gutters to the foot.

"Now and then," Red said. "A little wager can spice things up a bit."

Landry reached into his pocket, unpeeled a dollar bill from his hand. "I'm not talking high stakes," he said. "Beer money."

"Beer money it is," Red said, tossing a dollar bill on the table.

Landry tipped his glass and emptied it in a few gulps, then refreshed it from the pitcher.

Red walked around the table and began setting up the rack. "Is there anything exciting to do in this town," he asked as nonchalantly as he could. "Cards, craps, that kind of thing? Hell, I'd even settle for a cockfight." He laughed like the last part was a joke, then leaned over for the break. The cue collided with a loud crack, sending balls in every direction, sinking the ten exactly where he'd hoped.

Landry didn't say anything at first, but instead shook himself, like someone had dropped an ice cube down his shirt. "Cockfights," he said. "My stomach can't take that shit."

Red stretched the stick over the felt, moving it from one position to another, scoping possibilities. He paused and looked over to Landry, who was staring intently back. "Something wrong?" he asked.

"Not wrong," Landry replied. "I'm just surprised is all."

Red tapped the end of his stick onto the floor. "Surprised about what?"

"Surprised that you got around to bringing up the cockfight so soon."

By the time the two men made their way back to the booth, Linda was sitting there alone, thumbing through a Little Nickel paper and picking at a bowl of peanuts. Pieces of discarded shells lay in a little pile on the table.

"Where's Ruby?" Landry asked.

"She called herself a cab about twenty minutes ago," Linda said. "She told me it was nice meeting us but that she didn't get all dolled up just to listen to you fellows knocking balls all night."

"Well, that's Ruby," Landry said with a laugh. "She loves the glitter and sparkle, but the minute she don't get the attention she wants, she hits the road."

Red slid into the booth next to Linda, Landry taking the seat opposite them. He snatched a peanut from the bowl. "We can cut the bullshit anytime," he said, cracking it in half. "I know who you are." He pointed a finger at Red. "But I don't know who you are, except to say that I'll bet your name isn't Caroline."

Linda smiled at him but said nothing.

"So, let's do this," Landry went on. "How about you tell me what you know, and I'll tell you what I know."

"About what?" Red asked, feigning ignorance.

"About what?" Landry laughed. "About Gina, man. About your daughter."

Red took a drink from the beer in front of him. There was a knot in his gut that told him that he ought to keep quiet, but every other part of him seemed to realize that he had nothing to lose.

"I know there was a wreck," Red began, "that killed a man. Gina might have been the driver, I don't know."

"She was," Landry said.

"You know this how?" Linda asked.

He shot her look. "What else?"

"That's about it," Red lied.

They sat there for a good thirty seconds without speaking until Landry said, "You talked to someone at the sheriff's office. What did he have to say?"

"Pretty much the same thing. The guy went through the windshield, and Gina's vanished."

"And he didn't find anything in the car worth mentioning?"

Red paused, let the question tumble around in his head a bit. It was a good bet that Landry was alluding to the money, but Red wasn't about to go there. Instead, he simply said that Brody hadn't said anything of interest.

"Son of a bitch," Landry hissed. He ran his finger down the handle of his mug. "Well, somebody's lying their ass off." He took up the pitcher and emptied the last of it into his glass. "I know you've been to Junebug's. She probably told you that Gina had been living there."

Red offered a gentle nod. He didn't know where any of this was going. Under the table, Linda pressed her knee against his.

"She tell you about the cockfight?"

"She didn't," Red said. "I don't know that she knew where Titus took Gina that night."

At that, Landry snickered. "That old gal knows a hell of a lot more than she pretends to know." He took another drink of beer, and it was then that Red noticed the abrasions on the knuckles of his right hand. They were the kind of injuries that could have come from a slipped crescent wrench—or the hard crack of a fist against a jaw. "I'm gonna lay out for you what happened," Landry said. "And then maybe you can finally wrap up whatever business you think you have here and be on your way." He motioned to the waitress for another pitcher. "The last time I was in Reno, I got thrown out of this club for drunk and disorderly…Me and Titus Riggs, who I'd only met a couple hours prior. I guess you could say I was the drunk, Titus the disorderly."

The waitress swept past the booth, leaving a fresh pitcher in her wake. Landry nodded gratitude, then poured himself a fresh glass. "Anyway, I had twelve hours till checkout time and Titus hadn't secured a place to sleep yet. So I let him take the floor at the foot of the bed. The next day, I'm on my way back to my sister's in Rockview, with my newly purchased El Camino and Titus riding shotgun, smoking up the last of my decent cigarettes. Rosie—who, by the way is my sister, and yes, I know you already poked around the beauty parlor—wasn't so happy about it, but agreed to let Titus take the sofa for a week, not one day more." At Rosie's insistence, Landry made a few calls and eventually found a job for Titus on a Rhubarb farm up in Midvale. It was there, he told Red, that he hooked up with Gina. "I can tell you they were trouble from the start. I think they were too much alike for their own good. Fire and fire."

The more Landry drank, the more he had to say. He explained to Red that from what he could tell, Titus was the kind of fellow who was used to getting what he wanted, when and how he wanted it. From what Rosie had said, and what he later observed, Gina did not seem like the type of woman that welcomed being told what to do. "And I don't know what it's like being some kid's parent, but I'd guess that having that boy made her even less willing to bend to someone like Titus. I hate to say it, but I think his trip through the windshield probably saved her ass in the end." With this statement, he raised his glass.

"That's pretty harsh," Linda said.

"Lady," Landry replied, "life can be fucking harsh."

He went on, telling them how he'd been the one to mention the cockfights, and how Titus was very interested, especially in the logistics, the money, that kind of thing. Titus told him that he had been in and out of casinos and card rooms for years, but he wanted to know how something like that could be managed in a barn of all places. "I told him it was just a backwoods operation. It's not like there would be fifty grand in a wall safe someplace. Probably a few thousand, tops. There'd be a big moose of a guy standing by a duffle. Probably a sidearm."

"You didn't find that odd?" Linda asked.

"Odd how?" Landry asked.

"That he was so hung up on the money?"

Landry shook his head. "Lady, if you've spent as much time around bettors and grifters as I have, you find it weird when people don't talk about money." He finished off what was in his glass. "Long story shorter," he said, "We met up here for a drink, then we all rode in Gina's car up to Quay's. Titus had her wait at the bottom of the hill, said we'd be back shortly. Then he walked his ass into that barn like he owned the place. Barely said a word to me, his eyes sweeping over the place like he's looking for lost keys or something. Pretty soon, he's nowhere to be found. I figured maybe he'd chickened out and left."

"Chickened out," Linda said with a laugh.

"The next match starts up and people are hollering and jumping up and down and losing their shit, nothing out of the ordinary. I went on out to look for Titus and made my way all the way down to Gina's car but still couldn't find him. I told her to hell with it all and I climbed into the backseat. But then all of a sudden, here comes Titus running down the hill, hollering at Gina to fire up the engine, with a pack of guys on his heels." According to Landry, Gina managed to tear out of there before the men in pursuit could reach the car. They drove Landry back to Shorty's and dumped him off at his El Camino, and that was the last time he saw either Titus or the Valiant in one piece.

"But what about the money," Red asked.

"She swears up and down she didn't take it," Landry said.

"So, you've seen her then," Linda said. "Since the crash."

Landry paused, his face suddenly flushed red. He finished his beer and starred into the empty bottom of the glass. "I figure if she didn't take the money, it means that deputy likely has it." He pushed air through his teeth, a string of spittle falling over his chin. "I wouldn't put it past the son of a bitch. It's probably the one thing keeping Quay and his kin from turning this county inside out to find Gina."

Red looked at Landry. More than anything, he wanted to take this guy by the shirt collar and shake him until his teeth fell out. He clenched his jaw muscles. "Tell me, is she okay?"

Landry picked up the nearly empty pitcher, waving it at the waitress standing over near the bar.

"She's okay," he said.

"And the boy?" Red asked.

Landry shrugged his shoulders. "I'm guessing he's fine. She keeps him pretty close."

The waitress appeared and took up the pitcher, pouring the remains into Landry's glass.

"How about we take a breather, cowboy?" she said to him. "Give your liver some time to catch up."

Landry put his hand on his chest and gasped, as if he was shocked at the mere suggestion. "The beer police have arrived," he said, reaching into his shirt pocket and unfolding a five-dollar bill. The waitress snatched it from his fingers and walked away with the empty pitcher. Landry waited until the waitress was clear on the other side of the bar. "If I was to take you to her," he said, "let you talk with her. Would you quit bugging everyone? Finally leave and take yourself back to where you came from?"

Red shot a look over at Linda, who told him with a mere tilt of her head that this was what he'd been waiting for the whole time.

"Yes," he answered.

# 16

Red slid into the passenger side of the El Camino, while Landry climbed into the driver's side. He fished a flannel shirt from the backseat. "Wrap this over your eyes," he said.

"Excuse me?"

"Make a blindfold. I don't want you to see where we're going."

"Jesus H. Christ, I ain't doing that," Red said. "And besides, that shirt stinks." It smelled like a combination of motor oil and some kind of animal.

"We ain't moving till you put that shirt on."

"Well, I guess we're not moving then, because the last thing I'm going to do is put that thing anywhere near my face."

They sat in silence for a good two or three minutes. Landry's stupid mustache inching up and down as he chewed his lip, like a brush cleaning the dust from the floor. "Christ almighty," he finally said. "But if my sister brings it up, you better say you have no goddamned clue how we got to her place." He fired up the engine and tore out of the lot, hooking a left and taking the road eastward, away from town. For the most part he stayed within the white lines, but Red reached down and cinched his seatbelt across his lap all the same.

The further they went out into the county, the less the notion of streetlamps seemed to be a thing. The headlights of the El Camino were dull and off-center, sweeping over the landscape as if seeing where you were going was a mere suggestion.

Red looked out the window at the tiny blossoms of yellow that popped up here and there—light from distant houses—and thought about Linda. He'd let her take his truck back to the motel, even though he didn't like the idea of her driving on unfamiliar roads alone—and if he was being honest with himself, he didn't like the idea of anyone else but him being behind the wheel of his truck. "So much for cloth napkins and candlelight," he had cracked to her before she left. She had wanted to follow them, concerned about how much Landry had had to drink, but Red told her that "he said it's me alone with him, or not at all."

Red reached over and wound down the window. As the wind poured in, a sudden burst of fluff kicked up from the floor of the car, whirling around the interior before being sucked out the open window.

"Feathers?" Red commented.

"Oh yeah," Landry slurred. "Once they're in here, they're impossible to get rid of. Like bedbugs." He let off the gas some, and Red noticed a lazy mailbox up ahead, leaning halfway to full collapse. The car slowed down to make a turn, no signal to think of and a wider turn than Red would have liked. The branches of several trees raked the open window as Landry found his way onto a narrow road. "Don't forget what I told you about how we got here," he warned.

They rolled over uneven gravel, nothing but trees and shrubs on either side of the road. Finally, the thicket cleared and the headlamp beams washed over the front of a two-story farmhouse. It was a smart-looking structure, with a covered porch and windows framed with shutters.

Landry brought the car to a stop and turned off the headlights. The darkness was sudden, and it was only then that Red considered that Gina was likely inside.

"It'd be best if we keep quiet," Landry said, his voice anything but. "I'm not in the mood for Rosie's third degree." They made their way up the porch steps, each board groaning under their weight. Landry produced a set of keys that may as well have been sleigh bells, for all the racket they made. He fumbled with the lock for a moment, then shoved open the front door with his shoulder. Red followed him inside. The interior was dark and cool and smelled of cigarette smoke and popup room deodorizer. "We'll sit here for a few minutes," Landry said, this time in a loud whisper. "I should probably eat something anyway." He slid his hand over the wall, and the kitchen was suddenly illuminated in an assault of fluorescent light, a bare, overhead hoop humming like a hive of bees.

The cabinets in the kitchen were likely original, a few cockeyed doors, all painted in a drab white with chips here and there showing a coat of yellow underneath. The handles were inconsistent—some knobs, a few drop handles, nothing to suggest they had been put on during the same stretch of time.

The walls were layered in a busy pattern of orange and yellow flowered wallpaper, mostly intact except for a few seams. Between that and the black wall-mounted telephone with an adjacent drugstore supplied calendar, and the analog clock with its electrical cord snaking down to the outlet, Red figured he could be standing in any postwar Americana kitchen. The only thing missing was a giant wooden fork and spoon set tacked to the wall.

Landry pulled a chair from the lone, round table and

motioned for Red to take a seat. He opened the refrigerator door and retrieved a can of Rainier. "Can I get you one?" he asked.

Red shook his head. "If it's all the same to you," he said, "I'd like to see my daughter."

"In due time." Landry's eyelids drooped, and he looked over at the doorway that led into the rest of the house. He put a finger to his lips, then pointed at the ceiling.

"It's late," Red said. "I came all this way at your invitation."

"I said…" Landry popped the top of the beer can. "In due time." He took a drink, and from behind Red came a croaking voice.

"What the hell is this?"

Red spun around to see Rosie standing in the doorway. She was wearing an oversized bathrobe, heavy and bunched at her feet. Her yellow hair flew in several directions, and she looked so different without all that makeup that Red might not have been able to pick her out of a lineup.

"Good evening, Rosie," Red offered.

"Oh, hell no," she said, shooting a sharp look at Landry. "You've got to be fucking kidding me."

"He found me," Landry insisted. "Like a goddamned mosquito. He wasn't gonna give up."

"No!" Rosie let her body fall against the edge of the doorway, clutching her head with her hand like she was acting out a scene from an old movie. "She's gonna lose her shit."

Landry ran his finger around the rim of the beer can. "She'll get over it."

"Oh, you think so? Why don't you be the one to tell her?"

"I will," Landry said. "As soon as I finish my beer, I will."

Rosie let out an exhausted sigh. "If you think she's gonna welcome you with open arms," she said to Red, "you're likely to be disappointed."

"I'm not expecting anything of the sort," he shot back.

"What exactly are you expecting? Showing up here in the middle of the night. It's not like anyone's been wearing out the doormat at that motel of yours, looking for you."

"So, you knew I was at the motel."

"I was aware, yes."

"What about Gina? Was she also aware?"

"What do you think?" Rosie snapped. "That she has no idea you're prowling around looking for her? Towns this small, you can't scratch your ass without someone picking up the phone to tell someone about it."

Red put his hands on the table and folded his fingers together. "I assumed anyone I talked to wasn't giving me the full story," he said. "Probably on the horn to her the second I walked out the door."

"And yet," Rosie said. "You're still here."

"She's my daughter," Red answered, his voice hardening. "And he's my grandson. What else would you expect?"

There was a sudden snorting sound, like the creak of a rusty hinge. Red looked over to see Landry, his head laid back and his eyes closed, mouth gaping like a fish. His chest rose and fell, the guttural sound of a deep sleep.

"Goddamn it," Rosie said. "Figures. He creates his own mess, drags it home and then expects me to deal with it."

"I'm sorry this feels like a mess to you," Red said. "My hope is that I can talk to Gina and square things away, and then we can head on back to the motel and be out of your hair."

Rosie glared at him as if she were stifling a laugh. "Don't count on Gina being willing to just up and go with you." She walked over and took the can of beer from the table, swirled it around a couple of times, then helped herself to a drink. She sat down in the chair next to Red. "I didn't mean you were a mess," she said softly. "Just…this whole situation. Plus, he doesn't tell me shit, just acts on impulse like he's done since as long as I can remember. Thinks he's doing something noble, then dumps it on me to figure out the details." She took another drink of beer. "Like that damned rooster," she said.

"Rooster?"

Rosie swiped her hand down her face. "He didn't tell you about the rooster?"

"Nope."

"Well, I assume you know about the cockfight."

"Yeah."

"He wanted to go. I told him not to—told him it wasn't for someone like him. Landry's soft with animals. He feeds strays. I once caught him putting an ice pack on a pigeon with a crooked wing. He's like that. I told him what cockfights were like. Brutal. How they fight to the death, and if they don't, someone finishes the job anyway. He didn't believe me. I don't know what he thought he'd see—maybe a couple of chickens in boxing gloves—but he went." She paused, rolling the can between her palms. "He didn't last long. Told me later he was standing in the back during the first fight, and immediately got sick to his stomach. He went outside for some air, walked around the building… and that's when he saw the barrels."

"The barrels?"

"Where they toss the birds after the fights."

Red winced.

"He was gonna head back to Gina's car when caught a glimpse of something moving. One of those damn roosters—still alive, barely. Landry didn't think. He just took off his flannel, wrapped the thing up, and took off down the hill."

"Jesus," Red muttered.

"Gina's there in the car, with no idea what's going on. Landry jumps in the backseat without a word. Then all of a sudden here comes Titus, yelling for her to start the car. He dives in, throws his bag in back, and just as she hits the gas," Rosie made a motion with her hands, mimicking chaos, "the thing just explodes. Wings flapping, blood and feathers flying everywhere. Gina's screaming, Titus is cussing, Landry's trying to hold the bird together in the backseat like he's got a grenade in his lap. By the time they got back to Shorty's, the thing had quieted down. Landry got dropped off at his car, the rooster still in his lap. That's what got the backseat all bloody."

Red recalled the blood spatter in the backseat of the car, the handprint. A wash of relief fell over him like a warm blanket. "What became of the rooster?" he asked.

"He's just fine. Struts around the yard pecking at the ground like he owns the place. He looks like hell and limps some, but he's good." Rosie pushed her lips out like a fish. "All right, Pops," she said. "Ready to make all hell break loose?"

# 17

It was downhill from the back porch to a wall of brambles, followed by a winding path through the brush to a small clearing, where the trailer—a little Shasta, striped yellow and leaning a little off-kilter so that the hitch rested squarely on a solitary cinderblock sat. From what Red could make out with just the single flashlight beam, there was no clear path to get to the trailer. It was likely that the thing had been in that spot for a decade or more, enough time for the perimeter of fir and juniper to reclaim the land around it.

"Hang back here," Rosie said. Red watched as she stepped over the pitted path to the door. She rapped on it with the butt end of the flashlight. "Gina, honey, it's me," she said. Rosie waited a few beats, then tapped again. "Gina? You awake?" There was nothing at first, until a horsey cough cut through the air, "I'm getting up."

Red had not been expecting the mere sound of her voice to hit him so hard. He realized how the little details had managed to peel away from his memory over time, that even a few years could erode things like tone and diction, how even when he tried his darndest, he couldn't bring the sound of Gretchen's voice to his ears anymore.

There was some rattling inside, and then the small door creaked open. Rosie kept the light aimed low so that Red could not see clearly see her standing in the doorway; nor, he imagined, could she see him.

There was a low murmur between the two of them, then the sharp cut of Gina exclaiming, What the fuck? as she stepped back into the trailer. Rosie appeared to reach inside as the flashlight beam danced around, the momentary whitewashing of windows and billowy drapes. There was more whispering between them, the tone bouncing from harsh to hush. Suddenly, the light swung from the ground to Red, hitting him in the face like a slap.

"Well goddamn it." The voice was like a hacksaw blade on metal, dry and hard and a hundred percent Gina.

"Do you want me to stay?" Rosie asked.

The response was unclear, but Rosie turned around. "Good luck," she said, brushing past Red and making her way back up the trail to the house.

He stood there quietly, allowing Gina to control the space for the moment. There was a Gibbous moon out, offering enough light to bring out the shadows and soft edges. From what he could make out, Gina looked to be thin and reedy, her hair pitched messily, probably from sleeping on it. There was enough light to suggest she was still coloring it blond.

"So, you gonna stay all the way over there in the dark?" she said finally.

"Not if I don't have to."

No answer for a few seconds, then "Well, it's not like someone tied you to a tree."

"Not yet, anyway," Red answered.

Another pause, and then, "You drove all this way to hunt me down like some dog. You might as well finish what you came here for." She reached up and fiddled with something overhead, and the porch lamp hissed to life. A flood of light washed over the side of the trailer, the ground, and Gina.

Red caught himself taking in a sharp breath of air, followed by, Oh. The bruise patched from one side of her forehead all the way down to her cheek, the whole thing swollen just enough to cause her eyelid to fall halfway. And what he'd thought was a part of her sleeve—as the moonlight had reflected on it strangely—was actually a bandage, wrapped like a mummy from her elbow to her wrist.

"You okay?" she asked him. "You look like you're gonna pass out."

"I wasn't ready for that."

"For this?" She gave a slight turn, letting the glowing mantle of the lamp sweep over her face and arm.

"Christ," Red said. "Tell me you went to the hospital."

She smiled at him, lifted her hand and turned her arm one way and then the other. "It looks worse than it is," she said. "Bumps and scrapes. Nothing broken."

"And the boy?"

"The boy?" she repeated, almost mockingly. "Noah, He's fine."

"So, he wasn't in the car."

"No, Dad. He wasn't in the car."

For the first time in days, Red felt as if he could breathe again. He walked slowly toward her and all that had been missing was familiar again. The way her lips drew down at the edges when she smiled. Those deep set, worrying eyes, the spitting image of Gretchen's. There was a part of him that felt compelled to take her in his arms, though he was unsure if that compulsion came from a place of want, or was merely something that should be expected of him. If Linda was there, she would likely be giving him a good shove.

"Where's your lady friend?" Gina asked, as if reading his mind.

He said nothing.

"You wouldn't believe how fast news travels in this place," Gina said with an easy laugh. "I got wind you were in town probably the second you checked into The Top Hat. You aren't the only person who's been looking for me and Rosie's not the only one working to keep me hidden"

"Her name's Linda," he said. "She's probably back at the motel by now. We separated at the roadhouse when Landry brought me here."

"You mean Shorty's?"

"Yeah, that's the place."

She coughed out a kind of laugh. "It's a special man that'll take his lady to a place like that."

Red bristled at the reprimand. He hadn't planned to have to defend himself, and had no desire to do so. A gentle wind picked up, the faint tinkling of wind chimes somewhere brushing through the night air.

"If you think I'm gonna ask you to come in, you're wrong," she said.

"I wouldn't assume anything."

"I don't want to wake up Noah. You've probably heard plenty about him, too." Gina stepped fully out of the trailer and closed the door behind her. She stood there for a second, as if waiting for him to say something more. A dig at her, or maybe a congratulations. But with Red keeping both options behind his teeth, she walked behind the back end of the trailer and returned carrying a folding chair. "You can sit down if you want," she said.

"Just don't let yourself get too comfortable," she warned. "I ain't looking to be out here bullshitting all night."

"That's fine, Gina," Red said.

"I just figured you'd be tired, is all," she added. "Being so old and everything." She cracked a faint smile, and suddenly, she looked more like Gretchen than she ever had. The curve of her cheekbones, tracing along her face to her chin—almost doll-like, Red told himself.

"So, go ahead, then," she continued. "Say what it is you came here to say."

And there it was. After all this time, the days of knocking on doors and passing her photo around, and imagining a dozen different ways it could go, here he was on stage with her. He had a million things he wanted to say to her, but only one thing he had to say.

"You can't just keep running, Gina." He leaned forward with his elbows on his knees and folded his hands together. "I'm afraid you're in a shitload of trouble this time. Leaving that accident like you did."

"You think I don't know that?" she snipped. "I'm not stupid."

"I never said you were. What I wanted to say is that I don't think it's so much trouble that it can't be dealt with. You just have to go in and talk with someone."

"Like always, you have all the answers, don't you? I know what I can deal with."

"A man is dead, Gina," he pushed back.

"Yeah, and that man you're talking about was a son of a bitch," she said, her voice rising a pitch. "Good fucking riddance, I say." She stopped then, as if she was waiting for Red to do something with what she'd said. Red considered it too, shaping the words in his head that he should say, as a father, and a grandfather, as the kind of man who ought to stand for what's right and what's wrong.

"What do you want to do?" he asked her.

For once, she had nothing to throw back at him. She reached a hand to her mouth, biting at her thumbnail, staring past him as if in deep concentration. "I'm not giving up Noah to the state," she finally said. "That's the first thing they'll do, you know. Take him away from me. Throw him in some foster home."

"It doesn't have to be like that."

"Oh, it doesn't? Are they gonna let me bring him with me to jail? Set us up in a little apartment?" She patted her hands over her jean's pockets, as if she was looking for something. Then she suddenly froze, locking eyes with him. "No way," she said with a laugh.

"What?"

"Don't tell me you're offering to take him."

Red could see in the lamplight the pools forming in her eyes. The creases on either side as her mouth pulled itself into a frown.

"Would it be so crazy?" he asked. "You know I'd do it. And then once you found your legs again, we could figure out the next steps. For both of you."

She stared down at her feet, shaking her head from side to side. She didn't want to hear it. Wouldn't listen to him.

"Gina—" he began.

"No," she interrupted. "You don't get to ride in here and be the hero, okay? I mean, where were you any of those times when I called you? Or wrote to you? When I needed just a little bit of your goddamned help? Where were you then?"

"I was always there, honey," he said. "I just…"

She raised a hand to quiet him. "You were always there, all right," she said, almost in a whisper. "Until you weren't."

"What do you mean by that?"

She let out a tired sigh, wiping at her eyes. "You were always there to track me down but by then I didn't want to be found. Where were you before that? Leaving me with mom all day so she could sit me in front of the tube while she emptied whatever bottle she had hid somewhere." She looked up at him then, her eyes blazing in the glow of the flickering lantern.

"Oh Gina," he said. "I didn't know. I guess I should have."

She shrugged her shoulder weakly, settled herself on the trailer steps behind her. "Maybe it's something you just didn't want to know," she said.

They remained there watching each other without talking, the faint outline of Gretchen standing between them once again. The silence around them was almost crippling. Even the chirp of insects would have been a welcome distraction, Red thought. Or the faint sound of wind chimes, which had stopped, or the distant barking of some dog. But there was nothing.

"Well," Gina finally said, "I'm done with this. I'm sure one of them will drive you back to the motel if you ask them to. Hopefully your lady friend made it back in one piece."

"I don't know about Landry," Red said. "He was passed out at the kitchen table when we left him."

"Ask Rosie then," Gina said. "If she wants you gone bad enough, she'll drive you." As she opened the door to step inside the trailer, Red asked her one more thing.

"Can I see him?"

Gina froze, keeping her back to him. "I don't…"

"Please, honey," he begged. "I won't bother him and I won't ask you for anything else. It's just…" he paused, searched for the words that might keep things in play. "After all this—it would be crazy for me to leave without even laying eyes on him. I promise, he won't even know I'm there."

She turned to look at him. "Oh Jesus Christ, fine," she said. "But don't make a sound. I don't want him waking up, and I sure as hell don't want him seeing you. It'll only confuse him."

Gina turned on the lamp, and the room was suddenly bathed in a warm light. The boy was curled up in bed, a stuffed rabbit at his side. Dark, ringlets fell over his forehead, apple cheeks round and ruddy.

"He's got your face," Red said. "Except for that hair, it could just as easily be you lying there."

She put her hand to her mouth to shush him, but it was too late, as Noah rolled over and stretched his arms out, opening his eyes and letting them fall squarely on Red. A strange sensation fell over him then, as if the whole world had suddenly gotten lighter. Noah sat up and rubbed at his eyes. He looked to Gina briefly, as if seeking reassurance, then back to Red.

"Noah, this is your..." Gina began, then paused. "His name is Red. He's momma's dad."

Noah rubbed at his eyes again, then crawled over to the edge of the bed.

"Goddamn it," Gina said. "He wants to say hi."

"Is it okay?"

Gina nodded, more a surrender than an agreement. Red went to the boy and sat down beside him on the bed.

"Hello, you," he said, touching the boy's hair. Noah lay down again, resting his head on Red's knee, his little face warm through the denim. Red put his hand on the boy's back and rubbed it, listening to the sound of his breathing, watching his chest rise and fall.

"Why, Gina?" he suddenly said, his voice almost a whisper.

"Why what?"

"All those phone calls, you were probably holding him right there on your lap—you never said a thing." Red kept his eyes on Noah, but he could feel Gina's stare pressing against him.

"I thought about telling you," she said, "But I knew that as soon as I did, you'd say 'Oh, Gina,' and that'd be it. I didn't feel like giving you one more thing to be disappointed with."

He looked up at her, at the map of shadows that obscured all but her eyes. "It wouldn't have been that way."

She pushed air through her teeth, like she was throwing his words back at him. "It's late," she said. "You should probably go."

"Gina—"

"It's late," she repeated. "He needs his sleep."

Red slid his leg carefully from beneath the boy and set him gently on the bed, getting up and moving to where Gina stood.

"He's seems like a good boy," he said. "And, I meant what I said."

She took his wrist in her hand and squeezed it. Maybe it was to silence him, he thought, or maybe it was her way of thanking him for ending the conversation where it was, that they could part at a moment that wasn't brought about by a fight.

"I'll call you," she said. "When I know what my next thing is. So you don't worry."

"I'd appreciate that."

She let go of his wrist and turned down the lamp.

"Can you find your way back up to the house?" she asked. "It's right up the path."

"Yeah, I can find it."

He leaned in, taking Gina in an embrace—or at least a semblance of one. As much as either would allow. She returned what she could in the way of a gentle pat on his back.

"Drive safe on your way back home," she said, pulling away. "I'll call you."

"Yeah," he said.

And then he left her there, closing the door behind him and making his way in the dark up the pathway.

Just as he came through the brush at the crest of the hill, Red was caught in a sweep of headlights, the rumbling sound of a car making its way up the drive. He couldn't make out what it was, but he had a pretty good idea.

"You got good timing." It was Rosie's voice, and he looked up to see her standing at the bottom of the porch steps. "Luckily she was still there at the motel," she said. "Landry's got no place behind the wheel and I sure as hell wasn't looking forward to making the drive."

"I appreciate it," he said as Linda's Volkswagen rolled to a stop behind the El Camino. She clicked on the dome light, giving him a little wave through the windshield glass.

"I'm sorry things didn't turn out the way you hoped," Rosie said. "With Gina. Whatever that was."

"I'm pretty used to things not going the way I want them to," he laughed. "But the effort is usually worth it."

Before Red left to go to Linda's car he said to Rosie, "You can call me. If things hit the fan hard enough, I'm in the book. Red Miller. I'm in Ash Falls."

"Yeah, I know," she said.

"Anyway, thank you," Red said. He let the words hang out there by themselves, with no residue of the countless lies she'd told him at their first meeting, playing dumb about Gina's whereabouts or even who she was. She'd done what she felt she had to, he supposed.

They held hands the entire way back, except when Linda needed to shift gears. Red told her the story of Landry and the rooster, which gave her a good laugh. Then he filled her in on what did and didn't happen with Gina, catching himself more than once when the details got caught up in his throat. He blamed himself, of course, as this kind of dynamic didn't just hatch in the moment, and he'd had years upon years to correct course and never did.

"She has to have known that the door's always been open," Linda said. "You can't force her to pass through it."

They passed an old church, its white steeple rising up above a low canopy of trees. Linda put on her turn signal even though there wasn't anyone around. She hooked a left and took the open road toward the lights of town.

"There was something about the fella in the car, though," Red suddenly said. "Titus. Gina made a comment about how she didn't give a damn what had happened to him, almost like he'd done something to deserve it."

"What are you saying?"

Red gazed out at the vast openness. He'd been dancing around the details in his mind for some time, the look of things at the crash site. The tracks. "There's just something about the way she talked about it that doesn't set right with me," he said. Every pebble beneath them, every fissure in the concrete found its way from the car's wheels, up through the seat and into his bones.

Linda kept her eyes on the road. He'd half expected her to finish his thought for him, to say what he couldn't seem to put together. Instead, she switched gears altogether. "What about the boy?" She gripped the wheel and leaned forward in her seat, as if the closeness to the windshield might help her see the world better.

"What about him?" Red asked.

"Well, did you get to see him? Is he all right?"

He meant to tell her yes, that he'd seen Noah, and that he was not only all right but that he was more than all right—beautiful, even. But it became caught in his throat and all he could do was nod his head. And it was then that he had the sudden feeling of a wave crashing over him, as if every tiny piece of the night—of the week—had collapsed down on his soul. He suddenly felt as if a giant weight had settled on his chest, the air coming to him only in short bursts. His heart seemed to beat through his shirt, and his stomach turned, feeling as if he was going to be sick all over Linda's car. He began to gasp for breath, winding down the passenger window to let the outside air in.

"Red," Linda called to him. "Red, honey, what's happening to you?"

There was a small clearing up ahead, a lone mailbox and weed-pocked driveway that led to a darkened house a good hundred yards or so back from the highway. Linda stopped the car and killed the engine just as Red threw open the door and stumbled out into the dark before falling to the ground on his hands and knees.

Linda came running, putting her arms on him, rubbing his back in wide circles. "Just let it out, honey," she said to him, her voice smooth and measured. "It's okay."

Red put his hands over his face and leaned back into Linda's arms. The warmth of her embrace cradled him as he fell to pieces, body shaking in spasms, tears and snot soaking his sleeve as he tried in vain to stop it all. "I don't know what's happening," he cried. "I'm coming apart."

"You're not coming apart," she whispered. "You're having a panic attack is all. Just try and focus on my voice. You'll come around."

They knelt like that, Linda counting numbers and talking about things like flowers and butterflies, until Red found his breath again and the waterworks stopped, and everything passed over him so that he could stand up on his own. Linda walked with him back to the car and they sat down on the bumper together. The sky above them was like the underside of a giant umbrella, near-black stretching from hills to mountain, a million stars blazing as sharp as ever. Pinholes in the umbrella.

"What the hell am I even doing?" he said. "What makes me think I could even pretend at being a grandfather when I could barely manage being a father. I must be out of my cotton-picking mind."

"Oh, stop it, now." Linda gave him a gentle smack on his knee. "You're as decent of a father as I've ever met."

Red shot a half-cocked smirk at her.

"Well, give me a little more time to come up with something better," she laughed, slapping his knee again.

He took both of her hands in his. "She was the one who brought up the subject of me taking him," he said. "And she laughed about it. Like the mere idea of it was a non-starter."

"Oh honey," Linda said. "That was her just trying to get out of the gate before you."

Red shook his head, drew in a heavy breath and let it out in a rush. "I just wish I knew when everything went so wrong," he said. "What I could have done to make things right again."

Linda leaned against him "It wasn't always just you and Gina, you know. There was a wobbly three-legged stool for a long time. From what you've told me, Gretchen had a hand in things."

"I know that," he said.

"Good," she said, giving him a squeeze. "I also believe that some people are just wired a certain way. Maybe nature made Gina a kid who could never settle down, who was always looking for something that wasn't there for her. I don't know. Maybe you were just two parents who did what you could for a tough kid, using what tools you had."

"I want to believe that," Red admitted. "I don't know."

"Believe it," Linda said, giving him a nudge with her elbow. "Think about all those times you spent chasing her. Even though you couldn't always bring her back, you went out there and climbed into that truck of yours and looked for her. And you're here right now, doing a heck of a lot more than a lot of folks would—more than the cops, even. And even if she can't speak to it right now, it matters that you cared enough to try. Because deep down, whether she wants to admit it or not, she'll always know it's true."

# 18

It was coming up on one in the morning when they pulled into the parking lot of The Top Hat. The area surrounding the motel, from the gas station to the funeral parlor on the corner, was dark and wrapped in what Red could only see as a cloak of loneliness. And yet, a trace of beauty existed, too, as if the entire world was sound asleep, fully at peace with itself.

"Should we let the night clerk know we'll be checking out in the morning?" Linda asked. "Is that still your plan?"

Red swept his hand through his hair, the feeling of dirt holding on to his fingers. It made no sense to stay any longer. He'd found Gina like he'd set out to do, and as he figured would happen, seeing her failed to do anything other than rile her up and push her even farther away. Like always.

"We don't have to tell them anything right now," he said. "I'll set the alarm. Get up early enough to get on the road before checkout time." The thought occurred to him that they might swing by the police station on their way out of town, to let Brody know they were leaving. But he didn't know what the hell he would say to him about any of it. He certainly wouldn't rat Gina out, and that would entail a footpath of lies bound to trip him up. Maybe it'd be best to just hightail it out of there and drop a phone call once he was back home.

They went past the office, where the college gal sat under the bare light bulb of the desk lamp with an open book in front of her. Linda was a few paces ahead of Red, her steps careful and heavy, every hour of her long day weighing down on her. It dawned on him that since she'd shown up that morning, they'd done nothing but race from one place to another. At least she'd sleep well, he told himself. She deserved that much.

He was about to say as much to her when she suddenly stopped in her tracks, turned and looked at him. Her mouth hung open halfway; her eyes were wide. From somewhere very near, the joyful squeal of a child.

Gina sat astride one of the reclining chairs on the pool deck. At the end of the chair were a couple of lumpy, black garbage bags. At the water's edge, where the steps descended into the shallow entrance, Noah crouched on his haunches. He was wearing one of those one-piece pajama sets, blue with stars all over it, the rear end padded and looking full. A purple ball just larger than a grapefruit floated just out of his reach, while Noah splashed at the surface, pulling the water toward him as the ball bobbed up and down.

"I didn't expect I'd beat you here," Gina said. She sat up and brushed her hands over the front of her jeans. A small smile crept from her lips. "Did you two stop for a nap along the way?"

"We stopped," Red said, remembering his panic attack. "How'd you get here?"

"Rosie brought me." She looked over at Noah and clicked at him like he was a dog. "Don't fall in," she warned him.

The boy looked back at her and in a clear voice, almost like a bird's chirp said, "I won't."

Linda let out a gasp as Red realized that this was the first time they had heard the boy's voice.

"Do you remember me?" Red asked him.

"Do you know who he is?" Gina said. Noah looked at Red and smiled. "Daddy?" he said.

"He's Mama's daddy," Gina corrected. "That makes him your grandpa."

"Pom-pa," Noah said. He kept his eyes trained on Red, screwing his face up like he was working on a puzzle. After a few seconds, he got up and toddled over to Gina, crawling up onto the chair beside her and burying his face in her shirt.

"He's shy," Gina said. Then to Noah, "You stink."

Then they all went silent, none of them knowing what to say next. Finally, Linda asked if anyone was hungry. "I have a bag of chips in the Volkswagen," she said. Then she suddenly burst out laughing. As if a fuse had been lit, Gina let loose a fit of giggles, leaning back in her chair and wiping at her eyes with her sleeve. Noah looked between his mother and Linda, a half-cocked grin on his face, eyes wide and unsure. Gina pulled him close to her, and he pushed his face into her shirt again, his smile peeking out from under the fabric.

"Oh dear," Linda sighed. "I don't know if it's the exhaustion or what, but it sure feels good to laugh." She reached over to Red and rubbed her hand on his back. "I'll go ahead and get those chips, then." She meandered back down the walkway, through the gate to the parking lot.

Red watched as Gina cradled Noah in her arms. As she ran her fingers through his hair and stared into the darkness past the concrete wall and over the adjacent rooftops, she seemed to be purposefully avoiding looking at Red, as if eye contact was something she could not risk.

"I take it you're here for the night," Red finally said. "You got your bags with you. I don't imagine Rosie's coming back to get you."

"I told her to just drop me off, and that I'd figure out what to do by morning. You think you can get a rollaway for the room?"

"I'll get you your own room," Red said.

"A rollaway is fine." Gina scooted Noah from the chair onto his feet and stood up, taking hold of the bags. "It's stupid to pay for a room when we're only gonna use it for a few hours."

By the time they got into the room, Linda was back with the chips. It didn't take but a crinkle of the paper for Noah to run over to her and plunge his hand into the bag. Red called the desk clerk for the rollaway, then sat down on the edge of his bed.

"You his girlfriend?" Gina asked Linda.

"Well..." Linda looked over to Red as if seeking guidance. "I suppose we could probably call it that now. What do you think, Red Miller?"

"I think I'm okay with the word," Red said. "Even though girlfriend sounds a little teenybopper."

Gina snorted. "Sounds serious." Then she looked at Red. "I'd like to say a few things to you. Before I do anything, I want to get some things clear." She shot a get out of the room glance at Linda.

Linda smiled. "I can take a book out by the pool," she said.

"I didn't mean to be a bitch about it," Gina said.

"You're not," Linda reassured.

"You think maybe you could change him?" Gina asked, motioning toward Noah. "Give him a bath?"

"I can do that. Does that sound good, Noah?" she asked. "Have a bath?"

Gina dug into one of her bags and produced a plastic duck, and one of those disposable diapers. "This nice lady's gonna run you a bath, Noah, while Mommy and Grandpa have a talk."

Linda took Noah's hand and led him into the bathroom. The door closed, followed by the rush of running water.

There was a tap on the door to the room, and the voice of the clerk telling them that the rollaway bed was outside. Red got up and wheeled the bed inside, unfolded it, and started to make it up.

"Don't," Gina said, taking the sheet from his hand. "I'll do it later."

Red put the sheet down, then took a seat opposite her on his bed. He folded his hands and waited as Gina took off her shoes and socks, then sat on the rollaway with her legs crossed one over the other—something she always did, and he could never do.

"I know you probably had it in your mind that you'd find me and that I'd tell you every detail you missed over the last however many years it's been," she began, "but I don't got nothing to tell. Just living day to day is all. I've been in Idaho for about a year, Oregon before that. That's all there is to say."

"What about Noah?"

"He's Frankie's, if that's what you want to know. I wasn't gonna keep him at first." She looked at the bathroom door. "But then Frankie said he wanted him. Of course, the second I get past the point of no return, Frankie decides to go out for a pack of cigarettes and—pow—disappears in a puff of smoke. How's that for a cliche?"

"He looks healthy," Red said, not wanting to talk about Frankie. "You're taking good care of him, from what it looks like."

"Well, it ain't easy," she said, her voice catching somewhere between a sigh and a scoff. "Everyone's got something to say about it, as if there's some kind of secret formula. Naps. Food. Timeouts or swats. Meanwhile, half the time I'm just trying to keep my eyes open and not throw shit at the wall...Noah's a good kid, but he's… constant. Sometimes I wonder if there's even a life outside everything that's him, if that makes sense." She let out a short, humorless laugh. "I used to look at Mom and think she was weak, but now—now I get it. There's a kind of tired that gets into your bones, you know? Makes you start thinking strange things. There's times when the idea of taking a long nap in the bathtub doesn't sound so crazy after all."

Red's knife-hand of a jaw tightened. "Jesus, Gina."

"What?" she said, too quickly. "It's a joke."

"Doesn't sound like one."

She shrugged. "Guess I'm not the funny one."

Red rubbed a hand across his mouth. He wanted to say something—you don't get to talk like that, not about your mother—but the words stayed inside him.

"I'm fine," she said, now her turn to change the subject.

"You sure? That's what your mother used to say."

A silence followed, thick enough to carry the whole weight of what neither of them dared to say aloud.

Gina reached down and took up her handbag, fishing through it and taking out a loose cigarette. Taking a lighter from her jeans pocket, she lit up. "I've decided I'm gonna go down and talk to the cops," she said. "Get this thing taken care of once and for all." She took a drag, then let the plume of smoke take up the space between them. "I'm sick of hiding and tired of running. I know they'll hit me with jail time. Maybe you could keep an eye on Noah, just till I'm out?"

"Are you sure you'd want that?" Red asked. "I mean, I could do it if you want. Linda already said she'd help out."

Gina's forehead arched suddenly like the opening of an umbrella. "So the two of you've already worked it out between you," she said, her tone sharp and clipped.

"Linda's good people."

"Says you."

"Says your father."

She took another drag from her cigarette and got up from the rollaway, walking to the window and pulling the drapes back. Even after that, her hands kept moving—picking at a scab on her thumb, twisting the frayed cuff of her jacket, rubbing the inside of her wrist—the same small rituals she'd done since she was a kid to keep from losing herself.

"I'm gonna tell you how it happened," she said. "So you can hear it from me." Her voice came out small and gunmetal. "No cops. Not...some deputy. You."

Red nodded.

"Rosie said she told you about the cockfights," she said. "And the money Titus took."

"And the rooster," Red added.

"Oh that," Gina said. This gave her a kick, as she laughed and shook her head. "Fucking Landry." She took another drag. "Anyway, I didn't know anything about the money. Titus said he was just going in to make a bet. He told me to wait in the car. But then pretty soon there's Landry in the backseat with that crazy rooster losing its shit and then comes Titus running his ass off down the hill with a fat bag in his hand and a half dozen dudes following behind. He barely got the door open before he's screaming at me to drive the hell out of there."

Gina said that Titus's plan was for her to drive him to Fresno, where an old buddy of his ran a wrecking yard. It was a twelve hour drive, so she'd have to stay the night once they got there.

She refused. "I was pissed. I told him I was gonna pull over and make him get out of the car. I said I'd call the cops and tell them he was trying to kidnap me. I was just rattling off all kinds of shit, whatever might make him give in."

"Did he hit you?" Red interrupted. "Is that—"

Gina shook her head. "I mean, he'd hit me before. Plenty of times. I'd hit him back. I wasn't afraid of him like that." She turned the cigarette over in her hand, like she was inspecting it. "It was stupid," she resumed, sitting back down on the rollaway. "No—worse. Not stupid. Crazy." She found the scab on her thumb and went at it again.

"What did he say?" Red asked. His voice was thin, careful.

Gina's face went flat, like a page left in the sun. "He said he could make sure Noah never saw me again." She swallowed. "He said he would call whoever and say I was unfit and they'd take him. And when I told him that was bullshit, that I'd already been down that road, he smiled at me. This really, creepy smile. And then he said he could get other people to take him. People that would do things to him—" She paused for a moment. "Then he put his leg against mine, like a brace. Like he wanted to keep me from slowing down. He flashed his hands at me and laughed when I flinched." Her own hands closed into fists so tight the knuckles went white. "I thought—he's gonna punch me. Maybe knock me out and then take the car. I thought he might..." The words came now in a rush. "So I...I reached down and tightened my belt. I could see this line of trees ahead and I—I just took it. I jerked—my foot—pushed down so hard. It—" She slammed the heel of her hand into her palm, a small, savage gesture. "I don't think I knew what I did till it was over."

Red felt the floor tilt. Of course he'd suspected this, in those quiet, gnawing days after the wreck. Walking through the site, the lack of skid marks and the clean path to the pines—that maybe she had done it on purpose.

"I could tell I was hurt, but not too bad," she continued. "I found him in the light between the pines and I knew he was dead. I went back and got the bag and took off. Got myself as far from the wreck as I could."

"So you have the money?"

"Yes, I have the money," she answered. "I didn't take it, but I sure as shit kept it."

"So you didn't plan it," Red said, trying to hold the line between his words. "You weren't trying to kill him."

"No. God, no," she barked. "It's not like I was thinking, I'm gonna kill him,. I just—when he mentioned Noah—and that creepy smile—I just thought, I have to stop this motherfucker. I thought if I scared him, if I did something—if I busted up the car, maybe hurt him a little bit—that I'd have time to get to Junebug and—" Her throat made a sound that could have been a laugh or a sob.

"Oh, Gina." Red said, his voice soft and unsteady. "If you'd died—if the crash had killed you—what then? Noah without a mother. Just like—"

Gina's face folded in on itself. She looked ten and thirty at the same time. "I know..." She seemed to be reaching for words, only to have them fall apart before they left her mouth. "Maybe I'm a coward, I don't know..."

Red wanted to scream that children were not something to be gambled with, that there had to have been other options. But he didn't know what those options could have been, and anyway it didn't matter now. The memory of Gretchen—gone one morning like a shadow pulled from a wall—pressed against the inside of his ribs. "You likely saved him from something," he said finally.

"I don't know what else you saved or lost. But I know you came back. You're here. That's what matters."

Gina's laugh was small and dismissive. "You don't have to pretend to be proud of me," she said. "I know what I did."

Red took a breath that was more a surrender than anything. There was no neat answer; there was only the questions of the night and the terrible fact that morning would require answers. "I don't know how to fix this, Gina," he said. "But I'm not walking away."

She looked at him, and for the first time since maybe forever, she let herself be quiet long enough that something like relief washed over her face.

Linda came out of the bathroom with Noah, the boy wrapped in a towel like it was a gown. "Clean as a whistle and almost a prune," she said too brightly.

Noah ran to Gina, the towel falling to the floor, and he crawled up onto her lap bare-assed as the day she first held him.

"My bed?" he asked, running his hand over the sheet. "Sleep here?"

"It's both our beds tonight," she said. "Let's get your pj's on, get you to sleep. It's gonna be morning before you know it."

"He can sleep up here in the bed with us," Linda said. "Is that okay?"

Red nodded.

"I was asking Gina," Linda said with a wink.

"I don't care," Gina replied. She dug into one of the garbage bags and pulled out a disposable diaper and cinched it up over Noah with the speed of a pro, then did the same with his pajamas. "Go on over to the big bed," she told him. "Get yourself back to sleep and we'll have a bowl of cereal in the morning."

Linda helped Noah get settled in the center of the bed,

smoothing her hand over his hair, then rubbing his back while his eyelids fluttered and drooped. Quickly, he was fast asleep.

Gina dropped the folded blanket onto the floor and spread out a sheet on the rollaway, then laid down on top of it, fully clothed.

"You gonna be okay there?" Red asked her. "Don't you want to take a shower or anything?"

"I'm fine," she said. "I'll take one in the morning before we go."

"Oh, hang on," Red said. He went over to his suitcase and picked out a lumpy T-shirt, then peeled back the shirt and produced the scruffy green dog. "I thought you might want this," he said.

"Oh, for Christ's sake!" Gina exclaimed, the beginnings of a smile crossing her lips. "I'd wondered what happened to her." She took the dog from him and looked it over. "She's kind of a mess."

"Chicken blood," Red clarified. "She'll clean, though." He took up the blanket and unfurled it, stretching it out over the lower half of Gina's body. And when she didn't say anything but completed the smile she'd only hinted at, he patted the top of her head.

"I'm glad you came here," he said gently.

"We'll see," she answered.

He squeezed her shoulder. "Whatever happens tomorrow and thereafter I'll be on hand. Linda and me, we'll take good care of the boy, and when you're out—when you're ready—he'll be waiting for you."

"Yeah?" she said, her eyes welling up. "I don't know how long that'll be, though."

"It's okay, hon," Red assured her. "We ain't going anywhere."

She looked up at him, wiped her eyes, then rolled over onto

her side to face the wall, tucking the dog to her chest.

He and Linda quietly changed into their sleepwear, Linda draping herself in a baggy, oversized shirt, Red in the boxers and undershirt he'd had on all day. They said their good nights and crawled in on either side of Noah, who by know was breathing with the heartiness of an old man.

Pretty soon, everyone was asleep, except for Red. He lay there staring at the ceiling, at the shapes and contours that were in his mind. All of the people in the world he gave a damn about were there in that room, brought together by both intention and chance. In just a few hours they would come together one last time, at least as far as Gina was concerned. He would drive her to the station himself to meet with Brody, while Linda could help Gina with the public defender. He wasn't sure how that kind of thing worked.

As he felt himself finally sinking into sleep, the rhythm of Noah's breathing was like a wash of waves drawing him out to sea. He thought of Gretchen, floating on the surface with him, her body brushing against his as they dipped and rose together. He knew that she would agree—if they could share this together—that at least Gina was now safe, relatively speaking, and that the fates they'd imagined for her would be worlds better than the possibilities if she was out there in the darkness on her own.

# 19

"Red!"

The sound of his name pulled him from a deep sleep, like he'd been caught with a lasso, cinched and pulled tight. He pushed himself up. In his fog, the first thing that hit him was that there might be something wrong with Noah. He looked over at the boy, who lay there still as ever, breathing slowly, sound asleep.

"Red." It was Linda. She was sitting up, and she nodded her chin toward the other side of the room.

The rollaway was empty, the blanket folded neatly on top. On the pillow was an envelope, with writing on the front that Red could make out clearly from where he was. It was his name, in large, block letters.

"Where the hell is she?" Linda asked.

"I know as much as you do," Red said. His jeans were on the floor next to the bed, half-crumpled from where he'd stepped out of them the night before. He bent down, reached into one pocket, then the other. Empty. "Son of a bitch," he muttered.

"What?" Linda asked.

"My keys." He stood, already pulling a T-shirt over his head. "She took my damn keys."

He was out the door before Linda could answer, the chill of the morning cutting through his boxers as he stepped into the motel lot. A row of cars sat under the pale sodium light—Linda's Volkswagen, a dented Buick, a motorcycle—but no sign of his truck.

He turned a slow circle, hands on his hips, the asphalt cold beneath his bare feet. A single paper coffee cup tumbled across the lot, catching against the curb. Beyond that, nothing. Just the sound of a semi downshifting on the highway.

He stood there another moment, then headed back inside.

"It's gone," he said flatly. "Pickup's gone." His tone was surprisingly sanguine, as if the truck's disappearance was something that he had expected.

Linda looked at him for a long moment, then dropped her gaze toward the empty cot. "She really did it, then."

Red didn't answer. He went to the rollaway, picked up the envelope, and tore it open. The sound of paper ripping filled the quiet as Noah stirred on the bed beside Linda, rubbing his eyes, half-awake to a world already unraveling.

Red sat down on the thin mattress, the paper trembling a little between his fingers. His voice came out dry and worn, like he'd already read the words a dozen times in his head before seeing them.

"'Dad,'" he began. "'I know you're mad at me and probably not even surprised. There goes Gina again. Running away. I thought I was going to do the right thing, but all of a sudden I knew there's no way I could be locked up anywhere. I'm not mad at you for coming to find me or trying to get me to turn myself in. It's just you again, wanting me to do what's right.'"

He paused, rubbed at the corner of one eye, then kept going.

"'For anyone else who reads this, I want you to have custody of Noah. I think that's best, even though I'll miss him tons. Linda seems like a nice lady, so make sure you keep her around—hah hah. Tell Noah I had something important to do and I'll see him again when it's all done. I promise I'll send some money as soon as I can. Love, Gina.'"

Red looked up. Linda was holding Noah in her lap, the boy fully awake now, gazing up at her with that wide, unguarded trust kids are born with—like he'd known her all his life.

Red glanced back down at the letter. "'P.S.,'" he read quietly. "'I know you'll be a good dad to Noah because you were a good dad to me. I don't know why I'm the way I am, but I'm pretty sure it's not because of anything you did. You tried harder than a lot of dads would. I think Noah will be easier than me.'"

When he finished, Red sat for a long time, the letter sagging in his hand. The room was still except for the hum of the motel's old air unit, and the slow, steady breath of a little boy who had no idea the world had just shifted under him again.

They sat in that space for what seemed like forever, the three of them. Linda re-reading the letter, over and over, Linda rocking the little boy back and forth and humming something that Red could not recognize. Noah, saying nothing, but continuing to gaze up at Linda like she was an angel, or maybe a princess. Outside, there was the noise of the housekeeping cart rolling past the door, and the chatter of women. Numero tres. And then, Te escuché!

"No mention of the truck," Linda finally said.

"No," he replied, "The Red Miller from last week would be on the phone to the sheriff by now."

Linda ran her fingers through the thick curls on Noah's head, looking warmly down at him as he held his thumb in his mouth and stared back at her. "What's the Red from today thinking?"

"I don't know," he sighed, then he looked over at her, at the way she was smiling at him. As if she'd asked him a riddle and was holding on for the punchline. "You still want to be a part of this?"

"I already told you I'd be there and I meant it."

He nodded, swallowed back the soreness in his throat.

Linda leaned down to Noah. "What do you say we get you dressed, fellow. See what your mom left in that bag for you."

Without saying much more, they packed up what they had and piled it into the back of Linda's car, then loaded Noah into the backseat. There was no toddler seat, so Linda tucked the trash bag of clothing under his rear and pulled the seatbelt over him as best as she could.

"Mommy come?"

The words, simple as they were, caught Red like a pitchfork to a hay bale.

"No, honey," he said. "Not right now."

"We're going to go for a drive," Linda said. "You want to see where your grandpa lives?"

Noah shook his head, his lower lip trembling. His eyes began to fill, but he held it together. He leaned back and rested his head on Linda's arm. Red reached back and brushed his fingers through the boy's hair.

"It's okay, fella," he said. "Your mama had to go away for a while. But she knows where my house is. She can find it real easy."

Noah blinked a few times, a single tear splashing from his eye and rolling down his cheek. He reached up and wiped at his face, and Linda leaned down and kissed him on the head.

"You're a good boy," she said. "I can tell that right off."

The sheriff's station smelled strongly of pine cleaner and burnt coffee, and the sharp drift of spent butts, crushed into a nearby ashcan. Red sat beside Linda on a vinyl chair that gave a low sigh every time he shifted his weight. A muted TV played the morning news, all weather maps and traffic alerts, while an analog clock ticked the seconds by on the wall just above the receptionist's head.

"He'll be right out," the woman said. It was the same black-haired gal who had been there the last two times Red had come by, but if she recognized him, she held it to herself.

Noah sat on the floor by Linda's feet, rolling a toy car over the tile. Every few seconds, it hit the edge of Red's boot, and he nudged it back gently.

Deputy Brody appeared from down the hall, a clipboard in hand. "Mr. Miller," he said, nodding once before his eyes moved to Linda and the boy. "And company, I see."

Red got to his feet. "This here is my grandson, Noah. And Linda."

Brody's expression softened slightly at the mention of the boy. His eyes ticked from toe to head, then he turned to Linda. "You must be Grandma, then?"

"I sure am," she said, leaning over and hoisting Noah into her arms.

Brody smiled, looking over the boy once more. "Why don't we step back into the conference room, talk a bit?"

They went into the familiar room with the high windows, Brody motioning for them to sit, dropping into the chair opposite. Linda set Noah onto the carpet behind them, straightening a kink in his shirt collar.

Red took the envelope from his shirt pocket and slid onto

the table between them. "She left this," he said.

Brody raised a brow but didn't touch the envelope. "Left it where?"

"In our motel room. We—uh..." he stammered, looking over to Linda.

"We saw her last night," she said, leaning forward and putting her hands on the table. "She told us she was ready to turn herself in."

"I thought she meant it," Red added.

"We both did," Linda said, tracking a glance at Red. "But sometime in the night...I guess she just slipped out."

Red reached over and took Linda's hand in his. "When we woke up, she was gone. She left the boy and the letter."

Brody's face gave nothing away. He finally slid the envelope closer, unfolded the paper, and began to read. The sound of his thumb smoothing the creases filled the silence.

When he finished, he leaned back, exhaling through his nose. "You're saying she came to you, spent the night, and then left the boy?"

"That's right," Red said.

"You didn't think to call me when she showed up?"

Red's mouth twitched. "Didn't think she'd bolt."

"Not without him," Linda added, nodding her head toward Noah. "We figured if she was ready to do the right thing, well, we could all get a good night's sleep and come together in the morning."

"And you don't have any idea where she might've gone?"

Red shook his head. "None."

The deputy studied him for another beat, like he might be weighing whether to press charges. Then he looked down at the letter again. "You mind if I make a copy for the file?"

"Go ahead."

Brody stood, slid the paper into a manila folder, and started toward the door, then turned back. "You plan on keeping the boy with you for now?"

"That's the idea," Red said.

"Well," Brody said, rubbing a hand over his jaw, "since you're family, that's probably the best option. But we'll need to loop in Child Protective, at least informally. Get a temporary placement approval on record."

Linda looked up from where she was smoothing Noah's hair. "What does that mean exactly?"

"Nothing to worry about," Brody said. "I can make a few calls, talk to the case manager I know over at CPS. She's sensible—won't make a fuss over paperwork if the boy's safe and in family hands. I'll tell her you're heading back home, and she can schedule a follow-up visit there."

Red nodded, though his stomach tightened at the thought of someone inspecting his home like a crime scene. "You think that'll be enough?"

Brody gave a small, tired smile. "You've done right by bringing him in. That counts for something. We just have to make sure everything looks good on paper, that's all. In the meantime, I can probably scare up a few things for the trip home—a car seat, some toys, that sort of thing."

Linda squeezed Red's arm. "We'd appreciate that."

Brody glanced between them again, then down at Noah, who was now trying to balance the toy car on its roof. "He looks like he's in good hands." He tapped the folder against his palm. "I'll make a copy of this letter and get CPS on the line. Then you can be on your way."

"Thanks," Red said.

"Don't mention it," Brody replied. He extended his hand, firm and steady. "And if you hear from her—anything at all—you call me. Doesn't have to be official. Just a heads-up."

Red hesitated, then shook Brody's hand. "Yeah," he said quietly. "I'll do that."

Brody moved his head in a slight nod, then left the room, the door swinging shut behind him with a soft click.

Red sat back, rubbing his thumb along the crease in his palm. Linda reached for his other hand beneath the table, her touch light but sure. Noah's car bumped against his boot again, and Red nudged it back, his eyes unfocused, seeing a stretch of highway that seemed to run forever.

After a quick phone call with a CPS worker by the name of Darlene, and a few papers to sign, Red gathered a paper bag full of plastic cars, picture books, and loose building blocks, along with a fairly new car seat, and loaded them into Linda's Volkswagen. She climbed into the rear seat beside Noah and worked at the straps and buckles to make sure they were good and snug.

"I'll stay back here with him," she said, pulling a cardboard book from the bag. On its cover, a yellow train chugged up a steep hill, a gray cloud pillowing from its smokestack.

Red gave an "ok" with his fingers, slid behind the wheel and fired up the engine. Twenty minutes later, Rockview had vanished from the rearview, and Red felt a hundred pounds lighter, like the town had been a weight sitting square between his shoulders.

Before long they crossed into Washington and through Spokane, Noah having dropped off to sleep against Linda's lap well before the border. His little cheeks were red, and his eyelids fluttered as he dreamed what Red hoped were good dreams. Linda vacillated between watching the landscape roll by and gazing lovingly down at the little fellow's face.

"His eyelashes are so long," she said. "I'd kill to have eyelashes like that." She looked at Red through the rearview. "You've got good ones too, you know."

Red checked the mirror. They looked like eyelashes to him—nothing worth noticing.

Linda reached up and brushed the back of his neck.

"You're pulling my chain," he said.

"The hell I am." She laughed, then leaned back into her seat. She began to hum, a tune that was familiar to him but not clear. She had a pretty voice, one that she didn't share often enough. The tune moved from low to high notes, like a bird lighting from one branch to the next. Pretty soon she found the words, and it all came together for him.

*But I know I'm just his daddy for a day*
*He's much too young to realize, why mommy can't come home*
*And that she wanted things this way*

"Kitty Wells," Linda said when she finished. "I changed it a little."

"I like Kitty Wells," Red said.

"I know."

They began the long ascent up the pass, the Volkswagen's engine working overtime. Just on the downhill side of the crest, a lone gas station rose into view.

"I'm gonna pull off here," Red said.

"The tank low already?" Linda leaned over and looked at the gauge. Noah stirred in her lap.

"I'll probably top it off. Pick up a few snacks for the boy."

"And for me." Linda shook Noah gently. "Time to wake up

honey." She reached under the seat of his pants. "Feels like it's time for a change anyway."

They pulled up to the building and Linda took Noah into the bathroom on the side, while Red took care of the gas before going into the cashier. He grabbed a couple of candy bars and a big bag of chips.

"I was in here last week," he told the cashier.

The woman gave him a cursory glance. Everyone has been in here last week, her face seemed to say.

"There were some kittens out there," he said. "Any of them still around?"

"Far as I know," she said. "You wanna pick up a can of food for 'em? Seems to be the thing."

When Red came outside, Linda was already over at the blackberry brambles. She squatted down onto her haunches with Noah close by her side. He wiggled on his feet, almost ready to hop up and down.

"Looks like you found them!" he called out.

By the time he reached them, Linda had one of the kittens in her hands. Carefully, Noah reached out his chubby hand, letting the kitten brush its paw at him, kicking its spindly legs as Noah began to rub at its belly.

"They're a lot tamer now than they were last week," Red remarked. "And bigger."

"I suspect they've gotten a good amount of attention and food," she said.

Red crouched down beside Linda, and peered into the undergrowth of the blackberries. There was a flash of white, and a flurry of movement in the shadows. He popped open the can and set it down at the entrance, and two more little ones came out. He reached down to one and scrubbed it behind the ears. Noah squeezed in between him and Linda, brushing the kitten's fur in slow, careful sweeps, like he was afraid it might disappear. Red did not think it was possible for the boy's smile to be any wider.

They came down the west side of the mountain with the windows down halfway, the breeze blowing Linda's hair from her face as she stared out the window, occasionally looking at Red, stretching her arm out to rest her hand on his knee.

Noah was tucked into the space between them, an old sweater of Red's piled on his lap as the boy kept a careful watch on the sleeping kitten.

"It sure is a curious gift," Red said aloud.

Linda turned from the window. "What's that?"

"Something that gal Sadie said. A curious gift. It's when something you can't imagine taking on somehow it turns out to be..."

He stopped, searching for the words.

"A gift," Linda said, smiling. She smoothed Noah's hair, then reached over and did the same to Red. "I like that," she said. "A curious gift."

# ACKNOWLEDGMENTS

I'm grateful to those folks who read this story throughout its development, who pushed me to dig deeper and champion Red's journey from those first pages. Thank you to my writing group: Anjali, Maureen and Susan, and my brilliant mentor, Kent Meyers, who encouraged me to stick with it when I wasn't sure I could bring Red home.

To the amazing team at Ig Publishing, Robert and Elizabeth, for embracing this story and shepherding it to the shelf, and to Natàlia Pàmies for her beautiful cover design.

Finally, to my husband, Shayne: Thank you for your incessant, pestering questions about the book's progress over the last couple years, and the heartfelt reminders that not only was this a book that I could finish, it was one that deserved to be finished.

www.ingramcontent.com/pod-product-compliance
Lightning Source LLC
Jackson TN
JSHW082351050826
106251JS00002B/2
* 9 7 8 1 6 3 2 4 6 2 1 3 8 *